2/01

The Nighttime
Is the Right Time

The Nighttime Is the Right Time

A Collection of Stories

Bill Crider

Five Star
Unity, Maine

This collection is a work of fiction. Names, characters, places, and incidents are either the product of the author's imagination, or, if real, used fictitiously.

Five Star First Edition Mystery Series.
Published in 2001 in conjunction with Tekno Books and Ed Gorman.

Cover design by Carol Pringle.

Set in 11 pt. Plantin by Rick Gundberg.

Printed in the United States on permanent paper.

Library of Congress Cataloging-in-Publication Data

Crider, Bill, 1941–
   The nighttime is the right time : a collection of stories / Bill Crider.
     p. cm. — (Five Star first edition mystery series)
   "Published ... in conjunction with Tekno Books and Ed Gorman" — T.p. verso.
   ISBN 0-7862-3045-2 (hc : alk. paper)
   1. Detective and mystery stories, American. I. Title.
  II. Series.
PS3553.R497 N54   2001
813'.54—dc21   00-050310

Table of Contents

Sheriff Dan Rhodes has been very, very good to me. He's appeared in eleven novels (so far) and several short stories, has sold to paperback, book clubs, and large print. A couple of novels about him have even been published in translation in Italy. Here's one of his typical cases.

Gored

No one ever invited Sheriff Dan Rhodes to the annual Blacklin County Stag BBQ. It wasn't that no one liked him. The truth was that the Stag BBQ was something of a scandal, and everyone wanted to be sure that the sheriff ignored it.

And he did. He would never have been there if it hadn't been for the dead man.

The Stag BBQ was held at a different location every year, this year's site being the camp-house on George Newberry's ranch, about ten miles out of Clearview and just off a paved two-lane highway that ran practically straight as an arrow thanks to the fact that it was built on an old narrow-gauge railroad bed.

Rhodes pulled the county car up to a lightweight metal gate. There was a blue and white metal sign on the gate to let the world know that George Newberry was a member of the ABBA, the American Brahmin Breeders Association.

Newberry himself got out of a red and cream-colored Ford pickup and opened the gate. Rhodes drove through. Newberry closed the gate and got in the car beside Rhodes.

"I'll just ride down with you," he said. "I'll come back for the truck later."

Newberry was a big man, over two hundred pounds, very

little of which appeared to be muscle. The car sagged slightly to the side when he sat down.

"I'll show you where to go," he said. He pointed to the barn. "It's around that way."

He sounded nervous, and Rhodes didn't blame him. It wasn't every day that someone found a dead man on your property.

The road they were following wasn't much of a road after it passed by the dilapidated sheet metal barn. It was really just a pair of ruts through a pasture blooming with yellow bitterweed and goldenrod.

Every now and then the county car hit a bump, and Newberry had to take off his Western-style straw hat to keep it from being crushed against the roof. He wiped the sweat off his forehead with his blue bandanna and stuck the bandanna in his pocket.

"It's Gabe Tolliver," he said.

So it wasn't just any dead man, not some homeless drifter that just happened to turn up on Newberry's property looking for a place to rest for a day or so and praising his luck at finding the empty camp-house. No, it was a Somebody. It was Gabe Tolliver, who had been a loan officer at the largest of Clearview's two banks.

"What happened?" Rhodes asked.

"I'll let you be the judge of that," Newberry said. Though the car's air-conditioner was running full blast, Newberry was still sweating. His Western shirt had dark circles under the armpits. "All I know for sure's that Ben Locklin found him lyin' by a brush pile, and Bo Peevehouse called you on that cellular phone of his that he's so proud of."

Ben Locklin was a vice-president of the bank where Tolliver worked. Or *had* worked. He wouldn't be reporting on Monday. Peevehouse sold life and accident insurance.

Newberry was also a big man in Clearview. He owned three of the most prosperous businesses in town: two convenience stores and a video store.

In fact, that was what the Stag BBQ was all about. It was a chance for the movers and shakers to get together and drink a lot of beer, eat some BBQ and homemade ice cream, tell a few dirty jokes, and do a little gambling.

It was the gambling that no one wanted the sheriff to know about, though it was an open secret. If the men wanted to lose a few dollars to one another shooting craps or playing jacks-or-better to open, Rhodes didn't really see the harm in it.

But it seemed that this year there had been some harm after all, at least for Gabe Tolliver.

The BBQ was the social event of the year for the men in Blacklin County, and everyone who was anyone got invited. Everyone who was anyone and a male, that is. Women weren't allowed. Blacklin County was becoming more conscious of women's rights by the day, but Blacklin County was, after all, in Texas, where a great many men still believed that some activities just weren't appropriate for women. Maybe they were OK in Las Vegas, but that was different.

Rhodes looked over at Newberry, who was holding his hat in his lap. The businessman was wearing jeans and a pair of expensive-looking boots that were covered with dust. It hadn't rained in Blacklin County for nearly a month.

"Don't worry," Newberry said, noticing Rhodes' glance. "I haven't stepped in anything."

"I didn't think you had," Rhodes told him.

Rhodes figured he'd be the only man at the ranch without a pair of boots. He was pretty certain that he was the only sheriff in Texas who didn't wear them. But they hurt his toes and he couldn't walk in them very well, so he was wearing an old pair of scuffed Rockports.

The car went up over a low rise, and Rhodes could see Newberry's camp-house, painted dark green and sitting on top of a hill not far from a big stock tank and in front of a thickly wooded area that began about thirty yards away and ran down the hill. There was a four-strand barbed-wire fence around the camp-house.

"Any fish in the tank?" Rhodes asked.

"Bass," Newberry said. "A couple of the guys have tried it today, but nobody's caught anything. I caught a five-pounder last spring, though."

Rhodes wished that he'd brought his rod and reel along, but it wouldn't have been very professional to go fishing while he was supposed to be conducting a murder investigation.

There were white Brahmin cattle scattered out over the pasture, crunching the grass with their heads down or looking at whatever it was that cows looked at. Rhodes couldn't tell whether they were purebred or not. They paid no attention to his car.

"Nice looking herd," he said.

"Yeah," Newberry said, sounding a little distracted. "Kind of wild, though."

"Wild?"

"You'll see," Newberry said.

Rhodes saw when they got to the body, which was located just inside the woods. Gabe Tolliver was lying on his back, and there was a terrible wound in his stomach, as if a horn had twisted his insides. Black flies buzzed around the wound, and a couple of them were crawling on it near a curling brown leaf that stuck to the torn skin. Rhodes hadn't known Tolliver well, and what he'd heard about, he didn't much like. Tolliver was said to be a womanizer and a bully, and it might

10

have been true. But even if it was, Tolliver hadn't deserved to die like that.

"Did you call a doctor?" Rhodes asked Newberry.

They were standing over the body. Everyone else was in the fenced yard of the house, and Rhodes could almost feel their eyes boring into his back.

"Didn't see any need of a doctor," Newberry said. His face was white. "Not much doubt that Gabe's dead. But listen, Sheriff, as wild as those braymahs are, I don't think any of them did this. What about you?"

Rhodes didn't think so either. He knelt down by the body and shooed the flies away with his hand. There were wood splinters in the twisted flesh, and there was a sliver of bark on Tolliver's blue Western shirt. There was a dark stain by the back of Tolliver's head, and his hair was wet with blood. He'd been hit, probably before the goring.

Rhodes stood up. The trees were native hardwoods, oak and elm mostly, with a few pecan trees thrown in. There were several dead tree limbs lying near where Rhodes was standing and more in the brush pile near the body, but nothing that looked as if it had been used to kill Tolliver.

"Cows didn't do this," Rhodes said.

He looked around the area carefully. There was a place nearby where the ground was gouged up as if an armadillo had been rooting around, though Rhodes suspected that no animal was responsible. He'd have to get soil samples to be sure.

He turned to Newberry. "Let's get back to your camp-house."

Newberry looked glad of the chance to leave the body. They walked up a little cattle trail, and Newberry sidestepped a cow pie, the same one he had avoided on their way down to see the body. Someone had stepped in the manure earlier, but not Rhodes, which was surprising to the sheriff. Whenever he visited a pasture, he generally stepped in something within ten seconds of getting out of his car.

He stopped and looked down at the cow pie. There was another one just to the side of it, and that one had been kicked to pieces. Both were fairly fresh, and the one that had been shattered wasn't yet entirely dry.

"What was Tolliver doing in the woods, anyway?" Rhodes asked Newberry.

Newberry turned around. "I don't know. There's not any bathroom up there at the camp-house, so nearly ever'body's goin' to come to the woods once or twice."

Rhodes hadn't seen any signs of that kind of activity, and said so.

"Well, mostly people just go behind the tank dam. But I know some of 'em have come down here to get wood for the fire. Maybe that's what Gabe was after."

"Who's the cook?"

"Jerry Foster."

Foster ran a discount auto parts store. He was the one Rhodes wanted to talk to.

Just before they got back to the house, an armadillo shot out of the weeds beside the trail and charged through the goldenrod and bitterweed. Little puffs of dust flew from its feet. Rhodes had never understood how something with such short legs could go so fast. He wondered if he could have been wrong about the gouges in the earth near Tolliver's body, but he didn't think so. No armadillo had done that.

It was nearly five o'clock, but because it was the first week in October it wouldn't be dark for more than two hours. The shadows in the woods were beginning to deepen, but there was a pleasant glow to the light that belied the circumstances.

12

Newberry's cattle grazed peacefully in the pasture, unable to get near the house thanks to the barbed-wire fence.

Rhodes didn't have time to enjoy the deceptive peacefulness of the scene. He went to the county car, which was parked outside the fence. He opened the car door, got in, and called the jail on the radio. Then he told Hack Jensen, the dispatcher, to send the justice of the peace to Newberry's ranch. And an ambulance.

"You think an ambulance can make it up to that camphouse?" Hack asked.

Rhodes said that he hoped so. He didn't want to have to haul Tolliver's body out in the back of someone's pickup.

"I'll tell 'em then," Hack said. "You gonna solve this and be home in time for supper, or do you want me to call Ivy for you?"

Rhodes thought about the barbecue that Jerry Foster was cooking. He thought about bread soaked in barbecue sauce and about potato salad and pinto beans and cool, thick slices of white onion. He thought about homemade ice cream. And he thought about the low-fat diet he was on at home.

"You better call her," he said. "This might take a while."

The giant BBQ grill was made from three fifty-five gallon drums split in half and welded together end to end. There was a stovepipe on one end. Rhodes could smell the mesquite smoke as he walked over to talk to Jerry Foster.

Foster stood by the grill. He was taller than Rhodes' six feet, and he was wearing a chef's hat that had once been white but which was now mostly gray and stained with smoke and grease. He was also wearing an equally stained apron that had "Kiss the Cook" printed on it in red. Someone had used a black marking pen to add the word "Don't" to the front of the sentence and an exclamation mark at the end.

Foster opened the grill as Rhodes walked up. Smoke billowed out, enveloping them and stinging the sheriff's eyes. Rhodes waved a hand in front of his face to push the smoke away.

Coals glowed under the slow-cooked meat. Rhodes looked hungrily at the juicy pork ribs while Foster poked a brisket with a long fork. Satisfied that everything was all right, Foster lowered the lid.

"Still planning to eat?" Rhodes asked.

"I expect we will, but Gabe's dyin' has pretty much put a damper on the festivities." Foster had a raspy smoker's voice. "There's no need to let the meat burn up even if we don't eat it today, though."

Foster was right about the festivities. There weren't any that Rhodes could see. He looked over at a big oak tree by the camp-house. The ground beneath it was worn smooth and packed hard, but there were no craps shooters gathered there. Everyone was standing around in small groups, whispering and looking over at Rhodes and Foster.

The shaded tables under the other trees were clear of cards and poker chips, but Rhodes wasn't entirely sure whether the gambling had come to a stop because he was there or because of Tolliver's murder.

Also in the shade of the oak were three washtubs covered with thick quilts. Rhodes knew that the tubs would be full of ice and that under the quilts were hand-cranked wooden ice cream freezers. Rhodes hadn't had any homemade ice cream in years. The thought of its cold smoothness made his mouth water.

"What kind of ice cream is in the freezers?" he asked.

"Peach," Foster said. "Last of the Elbertas came in back in August, and my wife put some up in the freezer for us to use for the barbecue."

Peach was Rhodes' favorite.

"Did Ben Locklin bring you any firewood?" Rhodes asked.

"Nope." Foster pushed up his chef's hat and wiped his forehead.

"Who did?"

"I brought the mesquite myself, in my truck. Got it from my place. Newberry doesn't have any mesquite trees, or if he does you can't see 'em from here. You need some mesquite for the flavor."

"I wasn't talking about the mesquite," Rhodes said, thinking how the smoked ribs would taste. "I was talking about wood from the trees down the hill."

Foster gave it some thought. "Bo Peevehouse. Brian Colby. Hal Janes. Ben Locklin was goin' to, but he got a little sidetracked, what with findin' Gabe dead like that. There might've been a few more. I didn't try to keep up. They just dumped it on the pile and left it. I didn't look to see who brought it."

There was a little stack of twigs at one end of the grill.

"Looks like you're about out of wood," Rhodes said.

"Yeah. I've used most of it. But the brisket's about done. We won't need any more."

Rhodes supposed that was good, but it was too bad that all the wood had been burned, not that he'd expected to find anything.

"Any idea who'd want to kill Gabe?" he asked.

Foster readjusted his chef's hat. "Sheriff, you know as well as I do that half the people here've known each other since they were kids. They've got reasons to kill each other that go all the way back to high school, if not before. And the other half didn't like Gabe all that much. He wasn't bein' any too lenient with his loans these days."

Rhodes had heard the same thing. He left Foster and went

looking for Newberry, who he found talking to Bo Peevehouse.

"I need to talk to a few people," Rhodes told Newberry. "I'll do it inside if that's all right."

"Don't see any reason why not," Newberry said. "Who did you want to see?"

"I'll start with Bo," Rhodes said.

Bo Peevehouse, who had a cellular phone, also had the biggest TV set in Blacklin County, or so Rhodes had heard. He'd never seen it, himself. Bo had done very well in insurance, which Rhodes knew about in the same way he knew about the TV set, through Ivy, Rhodes' wife, who worked at a rival insurance agency.

Peevehouse had red hair that he wore in a spiky crew cut that Rhodes thought looked pretty strange with his Western garb. Bo's boots were dusty but otherwise clean. His hands were smooth and white. Not the hands of a cowboy.

"Did you see the body?" Rhodes asked him.

They were sitting at a small wooden table in the camphouse, which had only one big room with a concrete floor. The rafters were covered with antlers, some of them small, some of them having five or six points, and the walls held pictures of wolves, deer, mountain lions, and Rocky Mountain sheep. There was a cot in one corner, a fireplace with more antlers nailed to the rough wooden mantel, and some metal folding chairs.

"Nope," Peevehouse said. "I didn't see it, and I sure didn't want to. Ben Locklin threw up, they told me, and I would've done the same thing. I don't need to see any bodies. All I did was call your office on my phone."

He patted his shirt pocket, where Rhodes could see the slim outline of the telephone.

"Flip model," Peevehouse said. "You wanta have a look?"

Rhodes didn't. "You brought some wood for the fire?"

"Sure did. Somebody's gotta do it, and I figured it might as well be me. I don't mind working for my dinner."

"Who else brought wood up?"

Peevehouse didn't know. "I was busy shootin' di—I mean I was doin' somethin' else."

"Who do you know that might want to kill Gabe Tolliver?"

Peevehouse didn't want to talk about it. He looked at the antlers, at the pictures, and at the concrete floor. Finally he said, "Sheriff, you know what it's been like in this county for the last ten years? People haven't had much money, and when the bank was sold to that holdin' company a lot of the old guys who'd been there for years lost their jobs. Gabe held onto his, but he had to be tough to do it. He couldn't do business the way he had before. You might say he was foreclosin' on the widows and orphans, and the only people who could get a loan were the folks who didn't need one. There were plenty of people who didn't like Gabe."

Rhodes knew Tolliver's reputation. But the word was that Gabe *liked* being tough. Foster had already hinted at it, and Rhodes had been hearing it for a long time before that. That wasn't really what he was interested in.

"Anybody here today get turned down for money he needed to keep his doors open?" he asked. "Anybody here today lose a house or a car because of Gabe?"

Peevehouse shook his head. "Not that I know of."

"I didn't think so. Now what about other things? The kind of things that people get really upset about."

"I don't like to gossip, Sheriff," Peevehouse said. "When you sell insurance, you meet a lot of people and you hear a lot of stories. I don't pay 'em much attention."

He was looking at the fireplace while he talked. Rhodes figured he was lying.

"I think you should tell me if you've heard anything," Rhodes said. "I'll just find out from someone else."

"I guess you're right," Peevehouse said. He looked away from the fireplace and sighed. And then he told Rhodes what he'd heard.

Ben Locklin was five inches over six feet, but his hands were as small and soft as those of a teenage girl.

"It was a hell of a shock," he said. "Seeing Gabe lying there, like that, his stomach ripped open. I don't mind telling you I lost my lunch. It was a hell of a mess. Looked like he got gored by a bull to me, but I hadn't seen any bull down there in the woods, or any cows either. That's why I told Bo he'd better call you."

"You thought somebody had a reason to kill him?" Rhodes asked.

"Gabe was a good man," Locklin said, folding his arms across his wide chest. "I know what people think about him, but they think worse of me. I'm his boss, after all. I could tell him to do different if I wanted to."

Rhodes didn't really believe that. Locklin had been with the bank for twenty years, but everyone knew that didn't make a bit of difference to the new owners, who were probably planning to get rid of him as soon as they got more of their own men in place.

"I wasn't wondering about his business practices," Rhodes said. "I wanted to hear about his troubles with women."

Locklin looked at him.

"You know what I mean," Rhodes said. "He had a wandering eye, from what I hear."

"I don't know about that," Locklin said. "What my employees do on their own time is their own business."

"In a town the size of Clearview it isn't. I've already heard about it from Bo."

Ben waved a dismissive hand. "Gutter talk."

"Maybe. You've heard about it too, though, haven't you?"

"I've heard. That doesn't mean I believe it."

"That kind of talk gets under people's skin," Rhodes said. "Whether it's true or not." He told Locklin what he'd heard.

Locklin thought for a second or two and then admitted that he'd heard more or less the same things. Rhodes asked if he'd mentioned the talk to Gabe.

"Yeah, I said something. He told me to mind my own damn business, not that I blame him. Whatever he was doing, it didn't affect his work at the bank."

"And those men I mentioned, they had loans they'd missed a payment or two on?"

Locklin shrugged. "Yeah, I guess that's right."

That was all Rhodes wanted to know.

George Newberry was just as reluctant to talk as Peevehouse and Locklin had been, but when Rhodes told him that he'd already heard the gossip, Newberry gave in. He confirmed everything that Peevehouse and Locklin had said.

"But it's just gossip," he said. "Stuff you hear if you hang around a convenience store all day like I do. I don't know that a word of it's true. You know what it's like when stories get started."

Rhodes knew. But there was generally a factual basis for things, even if the facts weren't as juicy as the story that finally made the rounds of the entire community.

"Both those men went down for firewood, according to Foster," Rhodes said.

"Maybe so," Newberry agreed, "but that doesn't make them killers."

That was true enough, but it put them in the vicinity of the murder. Right now that was about all Rhodes had to go on, that and the gossip.

"Send them in," he told Newberry. "I'll talk to them together."

"You think that's a good idea?"

"Maybe not," Rhodes said. "But it's the only one I have."

Neither Hal Janes nor Brian Colby looked like a killer. They were young and skinny, and in their tight jeans and Western hats they looked as if they were just about to go to a rodeo and ride a bronco or maybe enter the calf roping event. Colby had a red and white bandanna tied around his neck.

They came into the camp-house and stood awkwardly until Rhodes told them to sit at the table. He stood by the fireplace and watched them.

Janes was a little taller than Colby, but Colby was a lot wider through the shoulders. Either one of them looked big enough to have killed Gabe without too much trouble. Colby's boots were dirty, but Janes' were spotless.

Both men were nervous. Colby fidgeted in the folding chair, and Janes rubbed his hands together as if he were washing them.

Rhodes gave them a few seconds to wonder about what he was going to ask them. Then he said, "I know that you both went down to bring in some wood for the fire, and I know that one of you killed Gabe Tolliver. What I don't know is which one of you did it."

"Jesus Christ," Colby said, standing up and knocking over his chair. It clanged on the hard floor. "You must be crazy, Sheriff."

"Lots of people think so," Rhodes said. "What about you, Hal?"

Janes was still sitting at the table, still dry-washing his hands.

"I wouldn't know about that," he said. "I think you're makin' a big mistake, though, accusin' two innocent men without any evidence."

"How would you know I don't have any evidence?" Rhodes asked.

Colby picked up his chair and sat back down. He looked at Janes and seemed as interested in the answer to the question as Rhodes did.

Janes gripped the edge of the table with his fingers, looking down at his nails. "The way I heard it, Gabe's just lyin' down there dead. Nobody saw him get killed, so there's no witnesses." He looked up at Rhodes. "Ben Locklin found the body, and he said it looked like a cow did it, or a bull. Said Gabe looked like he'd been gored."

"So there must not be any evidence of any murder," Colby said, more relaxed now and tipping back his chair. "Ben would've seen it if there was."

"Ben's not a trained lawman," Rhodes said. "He works in a bank."

"So did Gabe," Janes pointed out. "The same bank. Maybe they had a fight and Ben killed Gabe."

"Ben found the body, all right," Rhodes said. "He didn't kill anybody, though."

"Did you ask him?"

"I didn't have to," Rhodes said. "Now let me tell you what I think happened."

"It won't do you any good," Colby told him. "I didn't kill anybody, and I don't have to listen to you."

"Me neither," Janes said. "I don't see why you're pickin' on us."

"Because of your wives," Rhodes said.

"You son of a bitch," Janes said.

Colby didn't say anything. He just sat there and looked as if he'd like to be somewhere else.

"Tolliver was after both of them," Rhodes went on, ignoring Janes. He'd been called worse. "You were both behind on loans, and he was using that to get at your wives. That's the way he was. He'd promise a little leeway if the woman would meet him somewhere for a drink."

"I think you'd better shut up, Sheriff," Colby said.

Rhodes ignored him the way he'd ignored Janes and leaned an elbow on the mantel in a space that was free of antlers.

"I think it happened this way," he said. "One of you saw Tolliver going for wood and followed him down there. Maybe you already had in mind what you were going to do, but I don't know about that. Maybe you just wanted to talk to him, tell him to stay away from your wife."

"So what?" Colby said. "What'd be wrong with that? If he was messin' where he shouldn't have been, he needed tellin'."

Rhodes agreed. "There's nothing wrong with telling. But that's not what happened. Whoever followed Gabe got so mad that he killed him. Maybe there was an argument first, and maybe Gabe said a few things he shouldn't have said. I don't know about that, either. I do know that somebody took a tree limb and clubbed Gabe in the back of the head."

"That wouldn't look like a bull gored him," Colby pointed out.

"No, so someone tried to cover up. Not that it did any good. That smack on the back of the head couldn't be hidden."

"Maybe he hit his head when he fell," Janes said. "After he got gored."

22

"That's a good argument, but it's not what happened. If he hadn't been hit first, he would have screamed. Somebody hit Tolliver and then gored him with a tree limb. Maybe with the same one he hit him with."

"Where's the limb, then?" Colby asked.

"Burned up," Rhodes said. "The killer broke it up and took it to Jerry for firewood."

Colby didn't believe it. "Wouldn't Jerry have noticed the blood on the pieces of the limb when he put it in the fire?"

"Whoever killed Gabe jammed the limb in the dirt to clean the blood off," Rhodes said. "If there was any blood still on it, the dirt covered it up. Foster wouldn't have been looking for it."

"Sounds like you don't have any evidence, then, Sheriff," Janes said.

"Maybe not. But I know who killed Gabe Tolliver."

"Who?" Janes asked.

"You did," Rhodes said, stepping toward the table.

Janes shoved back his chair, kicked over the table, and threw Brian Colby at Rhodes.

Colby and Rhodes went down in a heap on the floor. Rhodes banged his elbow, and Janes ran out the door.

No one in the yard tried to stop Janes. They didn't even know for sure what was going on until Rhodes came running out after him.

By that time Janes had vaulted the fence and headed across the pasture. Rhodes knew that if Janes made it to the river bottom, about a mile away, they might never catch him. The bottom land was thick with trees and if a man was careful and knew the woods, he could stay in the trees most of the way across the state.

Rhodes knew better than to try vaulting the fence. He

valued the more delicate parts of his anatomy too much for that. He went through the gate, but that put him even farther behind Janes.

He probably wouldn't have caught him if it hadn't been for the armadillo. The armored mammal, frightened by Janes' approach, sprang up out of nowhere and shot across Janes' path.

It was too late for Janes to try to avoid the armadillo. He kicked it, tripped, and went sprawling in the bitterweed. The armadillo rolled a few feet and then it was on its way again. Janes got to his knees, but Rhodes reached him before he could get up, put an arm-lock on him and then slapped on the cuffs. After that it was easy to march him back to the camp-house.

They got there at the same time the ambulance arrived, followed closely by the J.P., another county car carrying Deputy Ruth Grady, and Red Rogers, a reporter for the local radio station who was looking for a good story. Rhodes figured he would get one.

It was nearly dark before things were straightened out, but no one left. They were all too curious to know the story, and besides, there was all that barbecue to eat, not to mention peach ice cream.

They were so eager to hear the story that they even invited Rhodes to stay.

Red Rogers tried to get Rhodes on tape, but Rhodes didn't want to talk for the radio. He wanted to eat ribs and ice cream.

"You owe it to the community," Rogers said. "You have to tell us how you knew that Hal Janes was the killer."

Rhodes could smell the barbecue, and he looked longingly at the ice cream freezers under their quilt covers.

"We'll save you some ice cream," Newberry assured him. "You go on and talk."

"Great," Rogers said. "So how did you know it was Janes?"

"His boots were too clean," Rhodes said. "He was the only one here with clean boots. Which meant that he'd cleaned them off. I think he stepped in a cow pattie on the trail and left a boot print in it. But he noticed the print and kicked the pattie to pieces, so naturally he had to clean his boots. Deputy Grady is looking around for his bandanna right now. I think she'll find it."

Rogers was incredulous. "And that's it? You knew he did it because his boots were clean?"

"That and his hands," Rhodes said. "You look at all these men here, they're dressed up in cowboy clothes, but they're not cowboys. They're bankers and salesmen and store-owners. There's not a calloused hand in the bunch. Janes didn't want me to see his hands because he'd scratched them up on the limb he used to kill Tolliver with. You can't fool with that rough bark like that, not without marking your hands."

"But what about hard evidence?" Rogers asked.

"We'll find that bandanna," Rhodes said. "And we'll find traces of bark in the scratches on Janes' hands. We'll find cow manure on his boots, too, in the cracks and crevices. He couldn't get it all off."

"But will that prove he killed Gabe Tolliver?"

"He had a motive, the means, and the opportunity," Rhodes said. "We'll see what a jury thinks."

There was more that Rogers wanted to say, but Rhodes didn't listen. Everyone was eating from paper plates heaped with ribs and brisket, beans and potato salad, and the covers were off the ice cream freezers. Rhodes wanted to get his share.

It turned out to be even better than he'd thought. The ribs were smokey and spicy, and the ice cream was so smooth and sweet and cold that he could have eaten a whole gallon.

It was too bad, he thought, that Hal Janes and Gabe Tolliver weren't there to enjoy it.

Another series character I enjoy is Bill Ferrel, a Hollywood pri-vate-eye who's never appeared in a novel. He's been in a number of short stories, however, including this one, which was listed in the "honorable mention" section of a big volume of "the year's best fantasy stories." I never thought of it as a fantasy, however.

Cap'n Bob and Gus

I think it was S. J. Perelman who said that Hollywood was a dismal industrial town controlled by wealthy hoodlums, or something like that. Maybe he was right. But it seems to me there are just as many rich lunatics as there are rich hoodlums. In fact, the guy who was bellowing at me on the phone was probably both.

I was trying to calm him down. "Mr. Gober, I can't under-stand a word you're saying. Maybe if you'd stop yelling."

"Goddammit, Ferrel, I'm not yelling! You want yelling? I'll give you yelling!"

He turned things up a notch or two. He sounded like a buffalo with a bullhorn. I decided there was no need trying to make sense out of things until he ran down.

It took about five minutes by my watch. When I was sure he was finished, I said, "Go over the part about the parrot again."

"Goddammit, Ferrel, have you been listening to a word I've said?"

"Yelled. A word you *yelled.*"

That set him off again. He pays me pretty well, so I guess he's got a right to yell if he wants to. He's the head of Gober Studios, and in 1948 his pictures grossed nearly as much as those of any studio in Hollywood. As best I could tell Gober was hoping to do even better in '49, but apparently something had happened to the parrot.

I didn't know what a parrot had to do with Gober's box office, and I didn't want to fool with one, but I'm on retainer to the studio. Usually that involves keeping some star's name out of the paper for having gotten boozed up and assaulted a cop or maybe having knocked up someone's underage daughter. I could handle that kind of stuff, but a parrot? I wasn't sure about a parrot.

And then I thought I heard something about a cat.

"Hold on there a minute, Mr. Gober," I said, trying to interrupt his semi-coherent soliloquy. "Did you say something about a cat?"

"Goddammit, Ferrel!"

He always seems to start off that way. Sometimes I think I should just go ahead and have my name legally changed to Goddammit Ferrel and let it go at that.

"Goddammit, Ferrel, haven't you been listening to me at all? This is not just *a* cat we're talking about here. This is *the* cat. This is *Gus*."

"Oh. Gus."

"That's right. Gus. And the parrot is Cap'n Bob. Cap'n Bob and Gus. They made us a hell of a lot of money last year, and now Cap'n Bob is missing!"

Well, it had finally happened. I'd always thought Gober was more stable than most of the studio heads I'd met, but now I knew I'd been wrong. He'd flipped his lid, blown his wig, twirled his toupee.

Cap'n Bob and Gus were cartoon characters. So how the hell could one of them go missing?

As it turned out, it was easy.

The way Gober explained it, Cap'n Bob and Gus were not merely cartoon characters. They were real. Gus was owned by one of the layout men, Lyman Birch, who'd brought him to work one day and showed him off to the other men in the cartoon studio. Not to be outdone, a backgrounder, Herm Voucher, drove home and got his parrot. It seems that kind of behavior wasn't unusual among the cartoon crowd.

Gober said that when the animals got a glimpse of one another, it was hate at first sight. The parrot flew off Voucher's shoulder and went for the cat like a P-38 after a Messerschmidt. The cat howled and took off through the studio, mostly across the tops of drawing boards and people's heads. There were animation cels, paper, and drawing pens flying everywhere, and one bald guy got severely scratched on the noggin.

The rumpus might have continued for hours if someone hadn't held a drawing board up in front of the parrot when it was coming out of a turn. The bird smacked into the board and hit the floor and Birch grabbed it. Took them another hour to find the cat, who was cowering in a supply room.

Inspired to near genius by that little fracas the artists and writers created the first Cap'n Bob and Gus cartoon, giving the parrot an eye-patch and a tendency to mutter sayings like "A-r-r-r-rh" and "Avast, ye swabbies." Matters progressed from there, with several Gus and Bob adventures following in rapid succession. "The Berber of Seville," with the Cap'n as an opera singing Arab who does Rossini as he's never been done before or since, won an Oscar.

The story about the cat and combative parrot was funny to me but not to Gober, who also couldn't understand his artists' and writers' continuing need for stimulation and motivation. They insisted that they couldn't write, much less draw, if the parrot and the cat weren't on permanent display in the studio. When inspiration flagged, someone would let the animals out of their cages, and things would get lively almost immediately. The artistic result would be something like "Cat-mandu," with Gus on the trail of the Abominable Snowman, who turned out to be an awful lot like the Cap'n. Or "Cat-O'-Nine-Tales," in which the cat played Scheherazade to the bird's smarmy King of India.

Gober might not have understood anything else, but he understood the result.

"And that's why you have to find that parrot!" Gober finished up.

What could I say? He was paying me, even if he wasn't paying me very much, so I told him I'd be at the studio in half an hour. Then I hung up the phone and got my hat.

I pointed my old hoopie, a 1940 model Chevrolet with a smooth vacuum shift, down Wilshire and turned right when I got to Vine. Eventually I got to Cahuenga and turned left. Gober Studios was located not far from Universal, though the layout wasn't as fancy. A guy I knew named Harry was on the gate, and he waved me on through without looking up from his copy of *Unknown Worlds*.

I drove right up to Gober's office. It was the nicest building on the lot, of course, and there were a couple of post-war Buicks, both of them big black Roadmasters, parked right in front. One of the cars belonged to Gober. I didn't know who the other belonged to. Maybe his secretary, who was undoubtedly paid a lot better than I was.

She was also a lot better looking: blonde, six feet tall and built like the proverbial brick sanitary facility. She also had a voice like Veronica Lake, so I figured she was worth every cent Gober paid her.

She was efficient, too. She ushered me into Gober's office almost before I got my hat hung up. Then she quietly faded away. I stood there ankle deep in carpet and looked at Gober.

Gober got up from his desk, which was polished walnut and about the size of a football field, and by the time the door had closed behind me he was heading my way.

"Goddammit, Ferrel, what took you so long? Let's get going."

He was about five-three with wide shoulders and hair that was slicked down on his head. If he used Brylcreme, he'd used about a dab and a half. He was wearing a suit that hadn't come from Robert Hall, and there was fire in his beady eyes. I could see that he was ready to get to the bottom of this parrot business.

I didn't move. "Get going where?"

He didn't even slow down. "The cartoon studio." He passed right by me, opened the door, and headed out. He looked back over his shoulder without stopping. "You coming, or not?"

I followed him and grabbed my hat off the rack. He was already down the steps and striding across the street. He didn't even look up at the two elephants that nearly stomped him.

I waited until the elephants passed and stretched my legs to catch up. "What picture are those from?"

"The elephants? Some goddamn jungle epic, one where Rick Torrance gets to run around for seventy-five minutes with his shirt off."

I'd seen one of the Torrance showcases. The guy looked a hell of a lot better with his shirt off than I did.

We went around Studio A, a cavernous aircraft hangar of a building, and I was having to struggle to keep up with Gober. For a guy with legs not much longer than most people's fingers, he could really move. It was a hot day, with plenty of that California sun, and I didn't feel like running. The pace didn't bother Gober, though. He did everything fast.

The cartoon unit was housed in a building in back of

Studio A, and frankly the building didn't look like much. There was a lot of wood, a shingled roof, and a bad paint job. Drop it in the middle of an Army base and it might pass for a barracks except for the sign on the door: "HOLLYWOOD HOME FOR THE CRIMINALLY COMIC."

Gober didn't seem to notice the sign. He bounced up the steps and threw open the door. Before it slammed into the wall, it was caught by a tall guy with thinning hair. After making sure it wouldn't slam, he let it go and put an arm over Gober's shoulders.

"Welcome to the asylum, boss," he said. "It's damn good to see you!"

When he took his arm away, I could see that he'd taped a piece of paper to the back of Gober's sharkskin. "KICK ME," it said in big red letters.

"Never mind the glad-handing, Birch," Gober said. "I've got a guy here who's going to find that damn parrot of Voucher's."

Another man came running up to join us. He was round and red-faced and even shorter than Gober. He would have been perfect for one of the seven dwarfs if Disney ever wanted to do a live action version.

"Cal Franks," Gober said to me.

"There's no need for anyone to look for the parrot," Franks squeaked, waving his arms. "We've got something better!"

"Get out of my face, Franks," Gober said.

"You might want to listen to him," Birch said. "He might have a point. We're used to having the Cap'n around to stimulate our brains, and now that he's gone, we're not getting much done. We need *something*, even if it's a cockatoo."

"A cockatoo is a much better bird than a parrot," Franks

insisted, heartened by the show of support by Birch. "More colorful, more—"

A chorus of voices interrupted him. "No cockatoos! No cockatoos! No cockatoos!"

The voices stretched out the *O* sound in the first word so that it sounded like "No-o-o-o-o-o."

I looked over Gober's head and past the two men standing in front of him. There were fifteen or so other guys gathered in the room, all of them chanting monotonously. "No cockatoos! No cockatoos!"

"Shut up, you goddamn clowns!" Gober bellowed.

He had a real talent for it. They shut up and stood looking at him expectantly. He grabbed my arm and pulled me forward for the introductions.

"This is Bill Ferrel. He's a private dick, and he's going to find that parrot. I want you all to cooperate with him and do what he says. He's the boss here now."

You could tell by looking that at least half those jokers were just itching to make some kind of half-witty remark that had to do with *dick* and *privates,* but they restrained themselves.

They were a strange-looking bunch, too. One of them was wearing an aviator's cap with the earflaps dangling down. If he was the bald guy who got scratched, maybe he was wearing it for protection. Another beauty was wearing a suit coat over a dirty undershirt. A couple of other swells were smoking cigarettes normally, but one had his stuck in his ear. Every now and then he'd suck in his cheeks and then exhale some smoke. Don't ask me how he did it.

One guy separated himself from the group and came toward us.

"Herm Voucher," Gober said out of the corner of his mouth.

Voucher was so skinny he'd have to be careful not to slip down the straw when he was drinking a malted, but he had an Adam's apple that would keep him from going all the way down. It was big as a softball, and it bobbed up and down when he talked.

"You've got to find Percy," he said. "We can't go on without him."

"Percy?" I said.

"That's the parrot's real name," Gober informed me. "Cap'n Bob is just a stage name."

"I get it," I said. "The bird has an alias."

"So does my cockatoo," Cal Franks said. "His real name's Diogenes, but his stage name's—"

"No cockatoos! No cockatoos! No—"

"Shut up!" Gober bellowed. They shut up. Gober turned to me. "Goddammit, Ferrel, you can see what I have to contend with around here. But it's all up to you now. You do what you have to do, and find that goddamn bird."

He turned on his heel and left. The "KICK ME" sign fluttered as he passed through the doorway, and then he was gone.

The room was suddenly completely silent. No one was looking at me, though no one seemed to be doing any work, either. One guy lounged against the wall reading a racing form. One, who was wearing a sword that looked like it might have belonged to Basil Rathbone at one time, rested his hand on the hilt and stared at the ceiling.

Then, very low, so that I almost couldn't hear it at first, a low murmuring of voices began.

"Sam Spade."

"Philip Marlowe."

"Mike Shayne."

"Sherlock Holmes."

"Boston Blackie."

34

The voices came from all over the room, and every one was different. I wondered if everyone there had studied ventriloquism.

"All right," I said. "Let's get something straight. You guys may all be geniuses, but I think you're nuts." I opened my coat so they could see the butt of the little .38 I wore in a shoulder holster. "And if anybody puts a 'KICK ME' sign on my back, I'm going to shoot his hand off."

"We wouldn't dream of doing a thing like that," Voucher said. "We want you to find Percy."

"That's what I plan to do," I said, without having a single idea about how I'd accomplish it or even if I could. "Who's in charge here?"

Lyman Birch smiled. "Did you say *charge?*"

The guy with the sword whipped it out of the scabbard and stiff-armed it in front of him at about a 45-degree angle.

"Charge!" he screamed, and ran straight at us.

Herm Voucher pulled me aside while Birch opened the door. The swordsman ran right on out and down the steps. I could see him heading in the direction of Studio A as Birch closed the door.

"I still don't see why you have to find that stupid parrot," Franks said. He was standing right beside me. I'd moved around a little, but he was on me like a stick-tight. "Diogenes is much better. He's better trained, he's—"

"No cockatoos! No cockatoos! No—"

"Shut up," I bellowed. I wasn't as good as Gober, but I was good enough. "I've had enough of this crap. Now tell me who's in charge of this menagerie. Is there a producer here?"

From the expressions on their faces, you would have thought I'd asked if Typhoid Mary was in the room. Then there was a lot of histrionic gagging, with people hanging their heads over wastebaskets and out the windows. I knew I must be on the right track. Everybody hates producers.

"You must mean Barry Partin," Birch said.

"He'll do. Where's his office?"

"Back there." Birch pointed to a hallway at the back of the long room where we were standing.

"Good. I'll talk to him first, and then I'll want to talk to some of the rest of you. Don't wander off."

I didn't wait for an answer. I crossed the room, avoiding the drawing tables and the men who didn't move out of the way, which was all of them. Hard to believe that I'd thought Gober was a lunatic. He couldn't hold a candle to these guys.

It was only when I neared the doorway that I noticed the cage on the floor. It was a wire cube about four feet on a side. A gray tabby cat slept on a mat inside. He was huge. Curled up like that, he looked like a black basketball. There was something greenish peeping out from under one of his paws, but I couldn't tell for sure what it was.

On the left side of the door, there was another cage. This one was on a stand, and there was a cockatoo in it. The cage was very clean except for a few dark splotches that had landed on the newspaper covering the bottom.

"Is this Diogenes?" I asked no one in particular.

"Yes," Cal Franks said. He'd followed me across the room, though I hadn't noticed him. I couldn't shake him. "He's quite a handsome bird, don't you think?"

"No cockatoos! No cockatoos! No—"

I wheeled around, digging under my coat for the pistol, but no one was even looking in my direction. In fact, everyone was bent over his drawing board, working busily. Those guys were good.

I turned back, but I didn't comment on the handsomeness of Diogenes. I left Franks there, or hoped I did, and went through the door to look for Partin.

I walked down a short hall, past a couple of rooms that were devoted to storyboards featuring rough drawings of Cap'n Bob and Gus, and down to an office that had a closed door. The nameplate on the door read "Barry Partin."

I knocked, and a man's unhappy voice told me to come in. I opened the door and saw a sad little man in a baggy coat sitting behind a desk that was a mere shadow of the one in Gober's office. The carpet matched the desk; it was mashed flat and worn almost through in spots. The only thing I liked in the office was the two pictures on the wall. One was of Gus and Cap'n Bob decked out as Holmes and Watson in "Catch as Cat's Can." The other showed Gus, his eyes bugged out and his hair ridged down his back as he confronted Cap'n Bob in "Who Ghost There?"

I looked away from the pictures to the man at the desk. "Mr. Partin?" I said.

His face was as baggy as his coat. "Yes," he said. "Who are you?"

"I'm Bill Ferrel. Mr. Gober wants me to look into the disappearance of the parrot."

"Thank God," Partin said. There was a look of genuine relief on his face. "I thought maybe you were a new animator."

I didn't blame him for looking relieved. If I'd been in charge of that passel of bozos, I wouldn't have wanted another one dumped on me, either.

"No," I said. "I'm not an animator. I'm just a detective."

Partin smiled and some of the bags in his face disappeared. He asked me to have a seat. "You think you can find that bird?"

I folded myself into an uncomfortable chair by his desk and told him that I didn't have any idea. "I don't even know what's going on. When did the parrot disappear? Who would have wanted him? Have you gotten a ransom note or a call?"

I'd left the door open when I entered the office; Partin got up and walked over to close it. He stuck his head out, looked down the hall, and then swung the door shut.

"Surely you can see it," he said, as he crossed the frayed carpet back to his desk.

I couldn't. I didn't even know what he was talking about. "See what?"

He looked at me as if he thought I was a pretty poor example of a detective. "It was Cal Franks," he said.

"Oh. The cockatoo."

"That's right. He's been trying to get me to hire that cockatoo for the past year. He says he's not insisting on a leading role for it, not yet. A supporting role would be fine to start, he says."

"But you don't believe him."

"Of course not. But what I believe doesn't matter. The whole crew's against him. They don't like him, and they don't like his bird."

The part about the bird I knew already. "Are they really that serious about Cap'n Bob and the cat?" I asked. "I didn't know cartoonists used models."

Partin sighed. The bags came back into his face. "They don't, not usually. But you saw those people. They're all crazy. One of them actually put a 'KICK ME' sign on my back just yesterday."

I wasn't exactly shocked. I said, "You're kidding."

"No." He shook his head sadly. "Someone actually did it. I would never have known except that Rick Torrance kicked the hell out of me in the commissary. He thought it was a riot."

I almost hated to change the subject, but I did. I said, "Tell me what happened on the day the bird disappeared.

What were the circumstances?"

"I don't really know. When we left on Monday afternoon, the parrot was in his cage. When we got here yesterday, he was gone."

Today was Wednesday, which meant that Gober had waited a day to call me. Maybe everyone had thought the parrot would come back on his own.

"What about the cockatoo?"

"Franks brought him in this morning. He said they needed a replacement for Cap'n Bob and they needed it now. They're supposed to be working on a new cartoon. 'The Maltese Parrot.' Gus as Bogart, Cap'n Bob as Sidney Greenstreet. Maybe you saw the storyboards."

I had, but I hadn't noticed the subject matter. "I guess 'The Maltese Cockatoo' just wouldn't work."

Partin shook his head. "It would work fine. I think. But I don't know for sure what's funny and what's not anymore, not after being around this place. I'd rather work with Rick Torrance and the elephants than those maniacs out there."

"Who was the last person to leave the building on Monday? It wouldn't have been Franks, by any chance?"

"I don't know. I went home early. I had a headache. I seem to be having a lot of them lately."

He looked like he might be having another one, not that I blamed him. I felt like having one myself.

"I want to talk to Voucher and Birch. Franks, too. Is there someplace private?"

He waved a hand to indicate his shabby office. "Nowhere but here."

"Would you mind stepping out while I talked to them?"

There was a look akin to fear on his face. "Go out there with . . . them?"

"Maybe you could walk over to the commissary, get a

cup of coffee. Take an aspirin."

"Aspirin. Yes. A fine idea." He practically jumped out of his chair. "I'll just go out the back way. You can call in whoever you want."

He was out the door and gone before I had a chance to say anything else.

I went out and called Lyman Birch. When he got there, I was behind the desk, so he had to sit in the chair. He ran nervous fingers through his thin brown hair and asked me what I wanted.

"Just a little background. How much does the studio pay you for the use of your cat?"

His mouth tightened. "Are you trying to insult me?"

"Nope. Just asking."

"All right." He attempted a smile and just missed. "I was just checking. They don't pay me a thing. I'm just glad Gus is able to help out."

"And Voucher feels the same way about his bird?"

"Naturally."

Birch tried to relax, but it was impossible in that chair. He ran his fingers through his hair again. When he did, I saw something that looked like scratches just above his wrist. He saw me looking and put his hand down.

"What about Cal Franks?" I asked.

"I wouldn't want to say anything about Cal."

"Sure you would. I hear that no one likes him."

"Cal's all right. Not a bad guy at all if you get to know him."

"And he's been trying to get his bird a job here. Why is that, if there's no pay?"

"Cal just needs attention. He's always hanging around, or hadn't you noticed that?"

I'd noticed. "So he thinks if his bird got famous, he'd get plenty of attention?"

Birch shrugged. "Seems that way to me."

"How far would he go? Would he do a birdnapping?"

"Birdnapping? That's a pretty good one."

I could almost see Birch's mind working on a cartoon script. Gus stealing Cap'n Bob off the perch and holding him for ransom, maybe. I tried to bring Birch back to the subject. I said, "Would he?"

"Huh? Oh, maybe. You saw the things that go on out there. Anything could happen."

Birch was right, and that was the trouble. How could anyone tell what that bunch might do?

"Who was the last one to leave the building on Monday?" I asked.

"What?" Birch snapped to attention. "Why do you want to know?"

"I want to know who might have been alone with the bird, especially if it was Franks."

"It wasn't Franks." There was a long pause, and then Birch said, "It was me."

Well, that gave things a different slant.

"I always hang around to spend a little time with Gus," Birch explained. "He lives here now, and I like to let him out of that cage every day for a while. He needs the exercise."

That was true. If Gus were any bigger, they could use him as a stand-in for one of the tigers in Rick Torrance's next picture.

"But there's a back door that goes to the parking lot," Birch went on. "It's supposed to be locked by whoever leaves last, but I may have forgotten on Monday. The watchman usually takes care of it later if we forget, but someone could probably have come in that way after I left. And I think one of the windows might have been open. It gets stuffy in here if you close all of them."

Partin had mentioned the door but not the window. I wondered for a second or two how much *he* liked Cap'n Bob. Then I remembered that Partin was a producer. He liked anyone, or anything, that made money at the box office.

"Was there anyone else who might have wanted to get rid of the parrot?" I asked.

"No one," Birch said. "We all loved that bird. He was a gold mine."

He didn't sound exactly sincere. "The bird didn't like Gus, though," I pointed out. "I hear that when the crew needed inspiration, all they had to do was open the doors to the cages."

Birch nodded. "Gus was terrified of that bird. But he always calmed down after being attacked."

We talked a while longer, but I didn't learn any more than I'd known before. The building was easy to get into, everyone loved Cap'n Bob, and Cal Franks had ambitions for his cockatoo. I sent Birch out and asked him to invite Herm Voucher in to see me.

While I was waiting for Voucher, I telephoned Gober's secretary and told her to have the watchman get in touch with me. She complained that she'd have to wake him, but I told her it was an emergency.

Then Voucher showed up. He practically had to duck to get through the doorway. He was even more uncomfortable in the chair than Birch had been. His eyes teared up when we talked about Cap'n Bob. Or Percy, as Voucher insisted on calling him.

Voucher had thought at first that the parrot might have gotten out accidentally. "One of the windows was open. He could have gotten out of the building, but he would have come back when he was hungry."

"But he didn't," I pointed out.

"No," Voucher said. "And he was such a gentle bird, a real treasure. There was never another one like him. And to think that idiot Cal Franks thinks Percy can be replaced by a cockatoo!"

"*No cockatoos!*" reverberated in my head, but the ringing of the phone cleared them out. I talked to the watchman, thanked him for his time, and turned back to Voucher.

"Do you think Franks had something to do with Cap'n, uh, Percy's disappearance?" I asked.

"I wouldn't want to say anything bad about Cal," Voucher confided, "but the truth is that he's just like a lot of stage mothers I've seen. He knows *he'll* never be famous, so he wants to make his bird famous instead."

"And what about Lyman Birch?"

"What about him?"

"He loved Cap'n, uh, Percy just like everyone else?"

"Why of course he did." Voucher's Adam's apple bobbed. "How could he not?"

Good question. I dismissed Voucher and asked him to send in Cal Franks.

Franks sat in the chair, and his toes dangled a few inches above the threadbare carpet. I'd been thinking about things, and I already knew what I was going to ask him.

"How did you know the parrot wasn't coming back?"

He was so startled that he almost fell out of the chair.

"What?" His face grew even redder than was usual with him. "What do you mean? I didn't . . . I mean, how *could* I have known? I don't know what you're talking about!"

He did, though, and I told him so.

"Sure you knew. Otherwise, you wouldn't have moved

43

that cockatoo into the cage so soon. Gober waited a day to call me about getting the parrot back, so he must have thought there was still a chance of that happening. Voucher thought so, too. But not you. You moved your bird right on in."

"I . . . I knew I could move him back out if Cap'n Bob came back."

"But you aren't planning to move him, are you? You might as well tell me about it, Franks. I think I know what happened. What did you do, come in by the back way to pick up something you'd left behind and see the whole thing?"

Franks' shoulders slumped, and he leaned back in the chair. His toes were farther from the carpet than ever.

"Yes," he said. "That's what happened. How did you know?"

"Never mind that. Just tell me your side of it."

He didn't want to, but he was going to. He couldn't hold it back any longer.

"You're right," he said. "Cap'n Bob won't be back. I saw it all. My car was parked around back on Monday. When I got in, I remembered that I'd left a book at my desk. I came back to get it, and that's when it happened."

"Birch killed the bird?"

"What? No, of course not. He wouldn't do that."

"Wait a minute," I said.

Obviously I didn't have it figured quite as well as I'd thought. I'd seen something green—a feather?—in the cat's cage. There weren't any other feathers around anywhere, so it wasn't molting season. Birch, by his own admission, was the last one to leave the building, and according to the watchman, the door had been locked. Nobody else could have come in.

So I figured that Birch had finally gotten tired of the humiliation dealt out to his cat and decided to do away with the humiliator. The scratches on his arm would have come from the parrot's claws. Maybe Birch had even let the cat play with the carcass a little after it was all over. Birch was also the only one supporting Franks' plea to let the cockatoo take the parrot's place, and since no one liked Franks, I inferred that Franks had something on Birch.

It seemed that I was right about the last part, but not about the first.

"The cat killed the bird?" I said.

Franks dug around inside his jacket and came out with a handkerchief. He wiped his face, but it stayed red. He wadded the hanky and replaced it.

"That wasn't the way it happened at all," he said.

Well, nobody's right all the time. But I was doing even worse than usual.

"Why don't you tell me what happened, then." I was tired of guessing.

"Like I said, I came back inside. I guess Birch didn't hear me. He was down on the floor, playing with his cat. I must have scared him, and he jumped back and hit Cap'n Bob's cage. The cage fell over, and—"

He stopped and went for the hanky again, but I thought I could get the rest of it.

"The parrot got out," I said. "And flew out the window."

"He got out, all right," Franks told me after he'd rubbed his face. "But he didn't go for the window."

Damn. I was going to have to turn in my P.I. license if I didn't improve.

"Where did he go, then?"

Franks put the hanky away. "He went for Gus."

"So?"

Franks shuddered. "So Gus jumped him."

45

"I thought the cat was scared to death of him."

"He was. But Cap'n Bob was a little addled. The fall, I guess. He miscalculated and went by Gus and hit the cage, got a claw hooked in the wire and couldn't get loose. It was what Gus had been waiting for."

"But he didn't kill him?"

"No. But it was awful. Cap'n Bob was squawking, and Gus was yowling and scratching. The feathers were flying, and the fur, too, let me tell you. Lyman was trying to get them apart, but he couldn't."

So that's where the scratches came from.

"Something must have separated them," I said.

Franks nodded. "Finally the Cap'n got loose somehow, and started flying around the room. It didn't take him long to find the window. And then he was gone."

"Didn't you go after him?"

"Sure we went after him. He flew over the fence and landed on a palm tree."

"Did you try to get him down?"

"The tree was on a delivery truck with two or three others. It was gone before we could do a thing. God knows where it is now."

"But nobody killed the bird."

"No. But we couldn't very well tell anyone what had happened. They would have blamed us. Gober might even have fired us. So we decided just not to say a thing."

"And you brought in your cockatoo. Whose idea was that?"

Franks gave me an indignant look. "Well, it wasn't mine. Lyman thought maybe we could get by with it, substitute one for the other, but you saw how they were acting out there."

No cockatoos! I thought.

And then I thought, *But why not?* This bunch was just goofy enough to go for it.

★ ★ ★ ★ ★

The whole maniacal assembly was looking at me expectantly as I stood in the doorway between the cages of Gus and General Joe, which was the cockatoo's stage name.

"I've cracked the case," I said.

No one looked more surprised than Birch. "You have?"

"That's right."

"Where's my parrot, then?" Voucher asked.

"Right there," I said, pointing to the cockatoo.

"Huh?" I think all of them said it at once. And then someone said "No cocka—"

"Hold it!" They held it. "This is *not* a cockatoo. This is Cap'n Bob in *disguise*."

"Huh?"

Birch caught on fast. "I *thought* that bird looked familiar," he said.

"Are you sure?" Voucher asked.

"Let the cat out," I said. "And we'll see."

Birch had to wake Gus first, but he finally managed to drag him out of the cage. There was a feather in there, all right. Birch and Franks had cleaned up, but they hadn't gotten that one.

Gus stretched out his front legs and spread his toes while his rear end went up high. He swished his tail a time or two.

"Now, Cal," I said, and Franks let the cockatoo out.

It was hate at first sight this time, too, and General Joe shot off the perch like a V-2. Gus sprang to a drawing board and then to the head of the guy wearing the aviator's cap. He hit a hanging light fixture as he jumped to another guy's head, and then he was back on the floor, scuttling under tables and upsetting everything while General Joe patrolled the airspace and waited for a chance to dive bomb him.

By that time people were cheering and whistling and clapping, and even Voucher believed that his parrot was back.

In disguise, of course.

When Gus cleared the tables and the cockatoo dived, I snatched up a drawing board and got it in his way just in time. He thudded into it and dropped to the floor. Franks grabbed him and stuck him in the cage. I didn't see where Gus had gone. Probably to the supply room.

Birch saw me to the door amid a general atmosphere of hilarity and relief. "The Maltese Parrot" would be finished on schedule, Franks' cockatoo would be a star (in disguise, since he'd be drawn as Cap'n Bob), Voucher had his bird back (also in disguise), and all was right with the world.

Birch thanked me and clapped me on the back as he wished me well.

When I got to the Chevy, I took the "KICK ME" sign off and threw it in the back seat before I went to tell Gober the good news.

Like Bill Ferrel, in the previous story, Truman Smith is a private eye. He lives on Galveston Island and has appeared in five novels and two stories, one of which is reprinted below.

Poo-Poo

It was two days after Christmas, and someone had stolen Miss Ellie Huggins' cat. Or so she said. I thought it had probably just run away. In either case, I didn't want to try to find it.

"It's like we have an obligation, Tru," Dino said. "She was our fifth grade teacher, after all."

Dino has a strange sense of obligation to the past. His uncles practically ran Galveston when it was a wide-open town, but when the Texas Rangers closed down the gambling, Dino didn't feel obliged to go into some other branch of the family business. Instead he sits in his house and watches infomercials on television. But when an old friend, or even an old teacher, calls about some kind of problem, he feels as if it's his job to set things right.

The trouble with that is, he often feels it's a lot more my job than it is his.

"I don't want to get involved," I told him.

I was sitting in my living room talking to him on the telephone. I didn't want to go outside. It was cold and cloudy, and it was raining. I could hear the water running off the house and sluicing through the oleander bushes that surrounded it. I was drinking Big Red from a twenty-ounce bottle, reading *The Beautiful and Damned*, and staying dry and comfortable.

"Remember the last thing you asked me to look into?" I said.

49

"Hey, it wasn't my fault that that turned out the way it did."

Dino had asked me to look into several things, and none of them had turned out very well. He continued to maintain that it was never his fault.

"Besides," he said, "it's only a cat. What could go wrong?"

Now I was *really* worried.

"I'll help you out with it," he said. "Partners, right?"

I'd recently made the foolish statement that maybe Dino should go to work for me. What I did involved gathering information on people, the kind of information that I now have access to right in my living room, thanks to the wonderful world of computers. Since Dino hates to leave his house, the job seemed like a natural for him.

"We'd have to get outside," I said. "You can't look for a cat indoors. And have you looked outside today by any chance?"

"I know it's raining, if that's what you mean. But this is Miss Ellie we're talking about."

He had a point, I suppose. Miss Ellie had been one of our favorite teachers a long time ago. Every day after lunch, she'd read to us: *The Adventures of Tom Sawyer, Heidi, The King of the Golden River.* I suppose I owed her something for that.

"And it's her *cat* we'll be looking for," Dino said. "You have a cat, too, remember?"

That wasn't exactly true. I lived with a cat, but that was as far as it went. Nameless was a big orange tabby who came and went as he pleased. He let me feed him regularly, and on days like this one, he spent a lot of time curled up on one of my chairs or the bed, which was where he happened to be at the moment. But he wasn't my cat. He pretty much belonged to himself.

50

"She really likes that cat," Dino said. "He's the only company she has."

I sighed, put a playing card in my book to mark my place, and laid the book on the floor by my chair.

"I'll pick you up in half an hour," I said.

We drove over to Miss Ellie's in my little Chevy S-10 truck. The rain drummed so hard on the roof that we couldn't hear the radio, and the truck wasn't as waterproof as Dino would have liked. Rain was coming in around the door on the passenger side and getting his shirt wet.

"You ought to have a new seal put around this door," he said, moving over a little closer to me.

"I didn't know it leaked," I told him. "Besides, I don't think a seal would help. There's something wrong with the door."

"We could've gone in my car."

"I didn't want you to have to drive all the way out to get me."

"I think you're just mad because I talked you into looking for the cat."

"Animals seem to bring me bad luck. Remember the alligator? Not to mention the prairie chicken."

"Hey," Dino said. "That alligator wasn't my fault. You got into that one all by yourself."

I noticed that he didn't bother denying the prairie chicken, however. But it was Christmas, or only a couple of days after it, so I decided to let bygones be bygones.

By the time we got to Miss Ellie's house, the windows in the cab of the truck were misted over. That was because the heater didn't work.

"You're really driving a piece of junk, you know that?" Dino said.

"I'm sure the huge fee I'll get for finding Miss Ellie's cat will take care of that. I'll probably be able to buy me a new Ford F-150 or something."

"You wouldn't charge an old lady for finding her cat, would you? It would be more like doing a favor."

"I knew you were going to say that."

Miss Ellie lived on Church Street down toward the medical school in an old Victorian house that looked as if it hadn't been inhabited since the hurricane of 1900. Either Miss Ellie hadn't decorated for Christmas, or she'd taken the decorations down already. Seen under the dark clouds and through the rain, her home could have passed for the House on Haunted Hill. All we needed was some thunder and a lightning flash or two. And of course a hill. There was no chance of that. Galveston doesn't have any hills.

"Maybe if we sit here for a while, the rain will let up," Dino said.

I smiled. "The eternal optimist. You can stay if you want to. I'm going to get this over with."

I opened the door and made a dash for the porch. I was wearing a jacket that was supposed to repel rain, but it didn't work very well. Wet weeds leaned over the sidewalk and slapped around my ankles.

Dino followed me. He was wearing an Astros cap to keep his hair dry. I don't think it worked any better than my jacket did.

There was an old swing on the porch, but most of the boards were rotten. I wouldn't have chanced sitting in it. The screen on the door was rusty and pulled away from the bottom at one of the corners. There were three or four holes in it, and someone had stuffed cotton in them as if that would keep the mosquitoes out.

I knocked on the door facing and waited, with Dino standing beside me, dripping onto the porch. After a while the inner door opened a bit and someone peered out from the darkness inside.

"Is that you, Dino?" a quavery voice said.

"Yes, m'am. And Truman's with me."

"Well, you two may come in, then."

The inner door swung wide. I pulled open the screen and stepped through. The house smelled musty and damp. There were no lights on anywhere inside as far as I could tell.

Someone that I assumed was Miss Ellie stood a couple of feet away. I couldn't see her face. She was short enough to be Miss Ellie, however. She came up to about my waist.

"Follow me, boys," she said. "We'll go into the parlor."

We followed her down a short, dark hall and turned left into a large room. Miss Ellie turned on a light, and I blinked.

There was no sign of a Christmas tree. The room was furnished with very old stuffed furniture with antimacassars on the backs of the chairs and the couch. Nothing in the room looked as if it had been sat on since Miss Ellie was a girl.

I could see Miss Ellie better now. She still wore her hair pulled tight at the back of her head and coiled into a bun, but now the bun was entirely white, as was the rest of her hair. Her face was lined, but it had been lined long ago. The truth was that she hadn't changed much since she'd been my teacher, thirty years or so earlier. I'd thought she was ancient then, but she probably hadn't been so very much older than I was now. It was a scary thought.

I shivered slightly, probably because the room was cold and I was wet.

"My, my, Truman," Miss Ellie said. "You've become very handsome. And you too, of course, Dino. It's so nice to see the two of you. I've talked to Dino on the phone recently, but

I haven't spoken to Truman in years."

I felt vaguely guilty, as if I'd been caught rolling spitballs in the back of the classroom. I cut my eyes at Dino, who was looking virtuous, the good little boy who put in calls to his old teachers in their dotage. If only Miss Ellie knew.

"You boys have a seat," Miss Ellie said. "Would you like some lemonade?"

Lemonade? Two days after Christmas? What I wanted was to get out of there. I said, "No, thank you, Miss Ellie."

"Very well, then. But do sit down. I want to tell you all about Poo-Poo."

"Poo-Poo?" I said.

Dino sat in one of the chairs. "Her cat. Somebody stole her, remember? We're going to find her."

"Oh, I do hope so," Miss Ellie said. She sat on the couch and looked at me, her blue eyes as piercing as they'd been when I was in the fifth grade. "It's so lonely without Poo-Poo in the house."

Poo-Poo, I thought. I'm going to spend the afternoon wandering around in the cold rain and looking for a cat named Poo-Poo. Dino would owe me big time for this one. I sat down and waited for Miss Ellie's story.

It seemed that Poo-Poo, a lovely calico, had a cat door and could go and come as she pleased. On cold, wet days, she generally pleased to stay inside, but she wasn't there because she'd gone out some time during the night and never come back.

"Poo-Poo always comes back in the morning," Miss Ellie said. "I can't remember a single time when she hasn't come in and had breakfast with me."

I wondered if Poo-Poo had a place set for her at the table, but I was afraid to ask.

"And you think someone took her?" I asked.

"That's right, Truman. Why else would she have missed breakfast?"

She could have been run over, died of natural causes, or run away from home. I looked at Dino, and I could tell he wouldn't like it if I said any of those things, so I didn't.

"When I talked to Dino," Miss Ellie said, "he told me that he'd be glad to look for Poo-Poo and that you'd be happy to help out. I hope it's not an imposition."

I looked her right in the eye and said, "Of course not, Miss Ellie."

Water began seeping through my waterproof jacket after about ten minutes of searching. My running shoes had been soaked by the time I'd taken ten steps outside Miss Ellie's house, and my jeans were clinging to my legs.

Christmas lights that hadn't yet been taken down were red and green blurs in the rain. Santa and his reindeer sat on one lawn, looking as if they wondered what had happened to the snow. I brushed wet hair off my forehead and started up the walk.

Dino was smart. He'd gone down the opposite side of the street, so there was no way I could get my hands on him.

I knocked at the door, as I'd done at a couple of other houses, and asked the man who answered if he'd seen a stray calico cat. He was wearing a pair of old khakis and a white undershirt, and he had a can of beer in his hand.

"You kiddin' me?" he asked. "I'm watchin' a ball game."

He shut the door in my face before I had time to ask anything else.

It was pretty much the same on the rest of the block. No one wanted to talk to me about a cat or anything else. There had been a number of burglaries in the area recently, I recalled, and I didn't blame people for being a little touchy about talking to some stranger with water-soaked clothes and rain dripping down his face. Nothing spoiled the holidays quite like having your presents or money stolen.

Dino had finished his side of the street with the same kind of luck I'd had. He came across and met me on the corner.

"See any little calico carcasses in the road?" I asked.

"Don't say stuff like that," Dino said. "You wouldn't want to be the one to have to tell Miss Ellie that Poo-Poo was dead, would you?"

"No," I said. "And I wouldn't have to be the one. You would."

Dino took off his baseball cap and wrung water from it, then settled it back on his head.

"I'm not going to tell her, no way. We've got to find that cat."

"Where?"

"There's the alley, and the next block over."

"You take the alley," I said.

The house in the middle of the block was dark and the yard was choked with weeds. Not far off the sidewalk there was a Realtor's sign leaning at a slight angle.

I don't pretend to understand cats, but I thought that a deserted house might have a certain appeal for a cat if she could get inside. There was a high board fence in the back, but fences like that don't matter to cats. However, I didn't see any broken windows or open doors that might have given Poo-Poo an entrance.

Still, I thought it was worth a look. I walked into the yard and all around the house, my shoes squishing on the rain-soaked ground. Not only were the windows unbroken, they all had screens. There was clearly no way inside the house, not even for a really sneaky cat.

I was about to go back around front when I heard something. I stopped to listen and I heard it again. It wasn't loud, but it was very clear. It was a cat's meow.

Most of the old Victorian houses in Galveston are built high off the ground, as was this one, and I couldn't see in the windows. So I went up onto the small back porch and called out at the closed door. I felt like an idiot, but I said "Poo-Poo? Is that you?"

There was another meow, very close to the door, which was solidly closed. You'd think that a house for sale would be locked up, especially one that clearly had very few prospective buyers dropping by and just as clearly had been on the market for quite a while. But I opened the screen and tried the door anyway. It swung open easily, and a cat streaked out between my legs, crossed the back yard like a bullet and disappeared over the fence.

"Hey, Tru!" Dino yelled from the alley. "I found her!"

I decided that I'd torture him before I killed him.

Miss Ellie was so happy to have her little Poo-Poo back that I relented and let Dino live. I even let him take credit for finding the cat. Why spoil the day for him?

This time Miss Ellie offered us hot chocolate and clean towels. I took the towel and turned down the hot chocolate. After we'd both dried off as best we could and listened to Miss Ellie tell us how wonderful we were and how grateful she was that Dino had found Poo-Poo, we left.

"Didn't that make you feel good?" Dino said before I dropped him off. "I mean, you were a big part of it, Tru, even if I was the one who found the cat. And you saw how happy Miss Ellie was. Something like that can really get you in the holiday spirit."

"Absolutely," I said. "It was better than watching *It's a Wonderful Life*. We should do it every year."

"You don't have to be sore just because you didn't find the cat. I gave you some of the credit."

"And I appreciate it. But what I need now is a long hot shower."

"Me too. See you later, Tru."

He got out of the truck and ran to his door through the rain.

I had the hot shower and ate a big bowl of Wolf Brand Chili for supper. I fed Nameless, read some more in my book, went to bed, and slept the sleep of the just. Until around two o'clock, when I woke up and couldn't go back to sleep. I couldn't figure out what was bothering me for several minutes, and then I knew what it was.

I told myself that I should have thought of it earlier, but I'd been angry with Dino, and I'd wanted to get out of the rain. The analytical part of my brain had been turned off. It was just too bad that it had to turn itself back on in the middle of the night.

The question was this: if there were no broken windows in that deserted house, no open doors, no holes in the walls, how had Poo-Poo gotten inside?

I told myself that there were plenty of ways. She could have gone down the chimney, for one thing. After all, it was the season for things like that.

Or some interested buyer could have looked at the house, with Poo-Poo sneaking inside while the door was ajar.

Or maybe there were holes in the floor, and Poo-Poo had entered the house from underneath.

I didn't really believe it was any of those things, however, so I got out of bed and found a dry pair of jeans. I thought about calling Dino but decided against it. He usually slept pretty late in the mornings, and he'd probably be groggy for hours if I could even rouse him at all.

It was much colder when I went outside, but the rain had stopped and the clouds were gone. Bright stars glittered in the black sky. I could hear the waves washing up on the beach, and I could smell the salty Gulf. I got in the S-10 and headed for town.

At one time, many years ago, Galveston had been one of those towns that never slept, but the gambling had come to an end, as had a lot of other things. Now at two-thirty in the morning, the streets were nearly deserted. There were no cars at all in Miss Ellie's neighborhood except the ones parked by the curb.

I stopped the pickup and got out. The night was quiet, though I could hear the faint sound of the surf from beyond the seawall.

There were no lights on in any of the houses around Miss Ellie's, but Christmas lights still flickered outside in the yards of a couple of places where the homeowners had forgotten to turn them off or had decided to leave them on all night and to heck with the electric bill. I didn't see a sign of Poo-Poo or any other cat. Probably I should have gotten back in the truck and gone on home.

But of course I didn't do that. I went to the back door of the house where I'd found Poo-Poo earlier, trying to be even quieter than a cat. I tried the door again. The knob turned under my hand, and I pushed against the door.

It opened very slowly at first, and then very quickly, so quickly that before I could even let go of the knob I was jerked inside the house.

I managed to drop to the floor and do a forward somersault, so the baseball bat that was supposed to hit me in the head swished over me and knocked the breath out of whoever had yanked the door open. It may have cracked a couple ribs, too if the yell the guy let out was any indication.

I came up on my feet, my bad knee almost giving way beneath me, and turned around just in time to get my hands up before the bat hit me in the face.

I would have been better off if I'd been wearing a fielder's glove, one of the bushel-basket-sized ones favored by the current crop of big-league outfielders, but as it was I managed to stop the bat a couple of inches from my nose and get a grip on it without too much damage to my hands.

I couldn't see very well in the dark room, but I figured that whoever was trying to bash my head in couldn't see much better than I could. I tried to wrench the bat out of his hands, but he was stronger and probably much younger than I was. I didn't stand a chance.

So I shoved backward and let the bat go. The guy swinging it stumbled awkwardly and tripped over his friend, who was still lying on the floor and gasping for breath.

I heard the bat clatter across the floor and bang up against the wall, so I made a dive for it. I got to it about a tenth of a second before someone else, but that was enough time to give me a little leverage. I snatched up the fat end of the bat and jammed it backward.

The butt smacked into something hard, maybe someone's forehead or cheekbone. There was a loud groan and the thump of a head hitting the floor. Now there were two people lying there, three if you counted me, except that I was sitting.

I stood up, keeping the bat in one hand, and felt along the wall for a light switch. When I found it, I flipped it up. The light wasn't bright, but there was enough of it to make me blink as I looked down at the two young men lying at my feet. They couldn't have been much more than sixteen, if that, and

I didn't feel especially proud of having put them where they were or of most likely having solved the burglaries that had been happening in the neighborhood.

One of the boys, for that's what they really were, was beginning to come around. He was holding his side and trying to sit up. Judging by the way he was looking at me, I was lucky that the two of them hadn't had anything more lethal than a baseball bat.

"Let us go, old man," he said. "Let us go, and we won't hurt you."

I wish he hadn't said "old man." I'm not that old, in spite of the way I sometimes feel. I don't even have gray hair. Well, not much.

I looked at his friend, who wasn't moving but who appeared to be developing a nice-sized knot in the middle of his forehead. He was lucky I hadn't hit him in the nose.

"I don't think you're going to hurt me," I said. "You're not going to hurt anyone for a while."

He gave me a practiced smirk. He'd probably get even better at it as he got older. He was one of the predators, one of the unhappy ones who couldn't really see anything wrong with taking whatever it was that he wanted from whoever happened to have it. Sooner or later, he would have tried taking it from Miss Ellie, or someone equally helpless, who resisted just a little too much, and the baseball bat would have become lethal indeed.

I knew that I probably hadn't changed his destiny, but at least I'd postponed it.

"How'd you find us, old man?" he asked.

"You shouldn't have let the cat in," I said.

He looked at me as if he thought I might be crazy. He said, "What're you talking about?"

I didn't bother to tell him.

★ ★ ★ ★ ★

"You just couldn't stand it, could you," Dino said to me the next day. "Just because I found the cat, you had to go out and be some kind of a hero so Miss Ellie would like you as much as she likes me."

We were sitting in Dino's living room, where his TV set was tuned in to an infomercial in which a man who didn't look much older than the two I'd turned in to the cops the night before was talking about how to become rich by placing small classified advertisements.

"I didn't do anything to be a hero to Miss Ellie," I said. "I like to think I'm a little beyond trying to impress my fifth-grade teacher."

"So you're saying I'm not?"

"Me? I'd never say a thing like that."

Dino watched the infomercial for a minute. I wondered what kind of small classified ads you'd have to place to become an instant millionaire.

"So how'd you know they were there?" Dino asked after a minute or so.

"I didn't. But I thought they might be there. Someone was going in and out of that house often enough to let Poo-Poo slip inside and the burglaries had all been right around that area. It was a good place to hide out and wait until everyone was asleep, then break into a house. They could even watch to see whether any of the neighbors left their houses for a visit or to go to the grocery store or to a movie."

"You think they might have tried Miss Ellie's place?"

"Maybe. She was alone and she would have been pretty helpless against the two of them. She would have made a good target."

"I'm glad you stopped them, then. And I guess I deserve a little of the credit, too, come to think of it."

"Sure you do. If it hadn't been for you, I wouldn't have gone looking for Poo-Poo."

"And if you hadn't gone looking for Poo-Poo, you wouldn't have found those two punks."

"Right. So you might want to drop by Miss Ellie's one of these days and tell her how you saved her."

"I don't think so," Dino said.

"Why not?"

He looked over at the TV set. "I'd have to go outside. I think I'll just give her a call instead."

"You be sure to do that," I said.

I remember the 1950s with great fondness, and I thought it would be fun to use that era as a setting. So far, mystery writers Bo Wagner and Janice Langtry have appeared in three stories, of which this is the first.

See What the Boys in the Locked Room Will Have

1

Outside, the rain fell softly from a heavy gray sky, but the only sound in the room was the clacking of the keys on the old Royal typewriter as Bo Wagner's stubby fingers danced over the keyboard.

Bo was working on the final chapter of another in one of the most promising series of detective novels the 1950s had yet seen, all of them featuring Sam Fernando, the Gentleman Sleuth. The scene was one that Bo regarded as obligatory in all the books, the one in which the suspects are gathered in one spot, waiting for Sam Fernando to explain to them the mechanics of the seemingly impossible murder that formed the basis for the book's plot and, not incidentally, to reveal all of them and to the no doubt completely bumfuzzled reader just exactly who had committed the heinous crime.

Bo was really smoking along, never glancing at the keyboard but instead keeping his eyes glued to the handwritten pages on the wooden typing stand beside the Royal. He typed so fast that it seemed a miracle that the keys didn't collide and jam. He was so intent that he didn't even seem to notice the statuesque blonde who was standing not six inches behind his chair, reading every word as it appeared on the clean white typing paper:

Sam Fernando leaned at his ease against the oak doorframe and looked over the suspects who were crowded into the study of the deceased Dr. Dorman. Mrs. Hutchings sat in the overstuffed leather chair near the desk, her black eyes darting left and right, her double chins quivering. Harley Montfort was on the couch opposite the desk, his long legs sticking straight out in front of him, his ankles crossed, while next to him Missy Tongate, her bright red hair a mass of timpting tangles, squirmed. . . .

"Just a cotton pickin' minute, there, Bo," Janice Langtry said in her soft Texas drawl. "What're you writin' here, a sequel to *Forever Amber*? Let's have us a look at this draft copy."

She reached out a hand big enough to fill a catcher's mitt and picked up the handwritten sheets. She shook them under Bo's nose. "Can you tell me where it says anything about any 'mass of timpting tangles?' "

Bo admitted reluctantly that he couldn't find such a phrase. "But—"

"Don't *but* me!" Janice said. "I know it's not there, and you know it's not there. You spelled *tempting* wrong, too."

Janice Langtry was nearly six feet tall, and she was wearing a man's crisply starched white shirt with the sleeves rolled up halfway to her elbows, faded Levi's with the bottoms rolled into cuffs, and black suede loafers with white socks. She was also wearing White Shoulders perfume, the scent of which always made Bo a little horny, not that he ever dared mention that fact to Janice Langtry. Her long blonde hair was pulled back into a ponytail and tied with a red scarf.

"And what about that *squirmed?*" she asked. "I bet you a

dollar the next word you were goin' to type was *deliciously*."

"Maybe," Bo said. "But—"

"I told you not to *but* me. You couldn't spell *deliciously* if you tried, anyhow. The agreement is that you type it up on the page just like I wrote it out by hand and not change a thing. Have you been readin' those Mickey Spillane books again?"

"Maybe," Bo said, "but—"

Janice put the handwritten sheets back on the wooden stand. Then she put her hands on her considerable hips and looked Bo right in the eye. A lesser man might have quailed, but Bo managed to meet her gaze squarely.

It wasn't easy. After all, he was sitting down. Even standing, he was nearly three inches shorter than she, and where she was neat, he was pretty much of a slob. His green shirt was wrinkled and there was a dark stain near the second button. Bo didn't know what the stain was. His jeans had a small rip in one knee, and his shoes looked worse than the ones the photographers had caught Adlai Stevenson in.

"I write the words," Janice said. "You just type 'em. That's the agreement, right?"

"Right," Bo said. He reached into his shirt pocket and brought out a crumpled pack of Camels and a folder of matches. He stuck a Camel in his mouth and lit it.

"Those things are goin' to kill you," Janice said, waving a hand in front of her face to shoo away the smoke.

"Hey, Mickey Mantle smokes these," Bo protested. "They soothe his T-Zone."

"That's Lucky Strike."

Bo let a trickle of smoke out his nose. "Nope. Lucky Strike's slogan is LS/MFT. 'Lucky Strike means—' "

"I really don't give a big rat's rump *what* it means. You're just changin' the subject. You're the plotter, I'm the writer.

67

That's the agreement. You don't change my words, I don't change your plots."

"I'm also the typist," Bo pointed out, trying not to sound defensive.

It bothered him more than a little that while his head teemed with plot ideas, he could hardly write a complete sentence without help. He had convincingly murdered people on stage during a performance of *Twelfth Night*, with the audience watching; in airplane cabins in full view of all the passengers; in classrooms full of students; in automobiles with all the windows rolled up and the doors locked; and in any number of other "impossible" places, including not a few very much like the study of the unfortunately deceased Dr. Dorman.

But the truth of the matter was that while he could plot like a demon, he couldn't write for spit. His spelling was loathsome, his grammar was atrocious, and his sentence structure was indescribable.

He knew all that, but he didn't like it, which was why he constantly studied the masters of detective fiction prose, like Mickey Spillane, a writer he greatly admired, hoping some of their stylistic magic would rub off on him. So far, none of it had.

Spillane's style was different from Janice's, of course, and probably not suited to the adventures of the Gentleman Sleuth, but it was exceptionally effective nevertheless, or so Bo believed. And besides, Spillane's books outsold the adventures of The Gentleman Sleuth by about ten to one. It never hurt to add a little spice to things, and that's all Bo had been trying to do.

"You're only the typist because you said you wanted to do it," Janice said. "I can type just as fast as you. Probably faster."

She was right. Bo stubbed out his Camel in the ashtray by the typewriter and rolled the paper from the machine. He crumpled it and threw it in the trashcan by the desk.

While he was rolling in a new sheet, Janice said, "By the numbers this time."

"You're the boss," Bo said.

Janice nodded, the ponytail bobbing. "You said it."

Bo began typing again. This time he didn't add any squirming or "timpting tangles." He tried to tell himself that he didn't really care about all that descriptive stuff anyway, but it would have been nice once in a while to have something of his own in the writing. What really interested him, however, was the mechanics of the plot, and that's what he was getting to. His fingers jumped over the keys:

> . . . *Missy Tongate brushed her red hair off her forehead. Ferdy Dorman was behind the doctor's old desk, trying to look at home but failing miserably. Detective Lomax stared at each one of them in turn, then looked at the Gentleman Sleuth.*
>
> *"I don't know what you're thinking of, Fernando," Lomax sneered. "You know as well as I do that everyone here was outside the room when they heard the shot that killed Dorman. And the door was bolted from the inside. The gun was on the floor beneath Dorman's body. It's a clear case of suicide."*
>
> *Sam Fernando smiled. It was a smile that seemed to infuriate Detective Lomax, who had seen it all too often. "That's where you are mistaken," Fernando said.*

"That's great, that's really great," Janice said. "The readers love it when Lomax does that slow burn. They know that Sam is going to drop the bomb on him one more time."

Bo turned around. He tried to avoid looking at Janice's breasts, which were quite close to him. He'd looked at them a tad too admiringly a month or so ago, and she'd belted him one right in the kisser.

"You really like that part?" he asked.

"I said I did, didn't I. Why would I lie?"

"No reason," Bo said, turning back to the typewriter.

The slow burn was Janice's idea, and Bo thought it was corny. He often wondered why the readers never seemed to get bored with it. If he were Detective Lomax, he'd retire or move to another city where he'd never have to see Sam Fernando's smugly smiling face again.

What Bo wanted to do was write a scene where his hero's nerves jangled with the kill-crazy desire to smash some greasy-haired hood's teeth down his stinking throat and rub his nose off on the filthy bricks of the nearest building. But of course he *couldn't* write it, and Janice *wouldn't* write it, so there they were.

"You see," Fernando explained, still wearing the smile that seemed to enrage Lomax and cause the policeman's face to grow almost purple and pointing to the window frame, "if the thumbtack had fallen to the outside, *then we would never have known the truth. But the killer obviously miscalculated. Therefore—"*

The telephone rang in the next room, and Bo stopped typing while Janice went to answer it. He leaned back in the chair and tried to overhear what his writing partner was saying. Her voice was muffled, and he could make out only part of it.

"Yes, we're busy," she said. "We're murbling on mumble mumble, and it's garble garble . . . *What?* . . . And in a murbled room? . . . You're sure about that? . . . Yes . . . Of course . . . We'll be right there."

Bo heard the heavy click as she hung up the handset. She came back into the study with a stricken look on her face.

"What's happened?" Bo asked. "What's the matter?"

"That was Lieutenant Franklin," she said.

Bo knew Franklin, of course. Every writer of mystery stories needed to know at least one good source of matters relating to police routine and procedure, and Franklin was theirs. He read each of their books to insure an air of something approaching authenticity, though Bo insisted that authenticity didn't really matter. His theory was that he and Janice were selling fantasy.

"From the way you look, I'd say he didn't call to talk about some new plot device he's dreamed up for us," Bo said.

Janice shook her head. The ponytail danced. "No. It wasn't that."

"Well, what was it, then?"

"He called to tell us that somebody's murdered Ray Thompson. In a locked house. In front of three or four witnesses. And there's no murder weapon to be found."

2

Bo Wagner was thirty-five years old, but, as Janice often reminded him, he had never grown up. Which was why they were zipping through the streets in a black chopped and channeled '49 Merc' and why Bo was wearing a red jacket just like the one James Dean had worn in *Rebel Without a Cause*. The radio was blaring "C'mon Everybody" by Eddie Cochran. The wipers swished rain from the windshield.

"Are they sure Ray's dead?" Bo asked, taking a corner on

two wheels. He worked the clutch and shifted smoothly down into third gear as the car straightened out from the turn. "Sometimes they can do wonders in the hospitals these days."

"Ray's dead all right," Janice told him. "That's what Lt. Franklin said. He was shot twice."

"Where?"

"Somewhere in the house. That's all I found out. I just said we'd get there as fast as we could."

They were on a long, straight street, and Bo mashed the accelerator to the floor.

"Not this fast!" Janice said. "Not on this wet street!"

Bo slowed down, but not much. He couldn't believe Ray was dead. There had to be some mistake, but it was pretty un-likely that Lt. Franklin would be wrong about something that important. If he said Ray was dead, then Ray was no longer among the living.

"C'mon Everybody" ended and was followed by a string of commercials. Then "It's Only Make Believe" came on.

"Guy sounds a lot like Elvis," Bo said.

"He wishes," Janice said, but her heart wasn't in it. Bo could tell she was thinking about Ray.

Ray Thompson had been among their earliest admirers. After the publication of *The Red and Blue Clue*, the first Sam Fernando book, Ray had called Bo.

"I just wanted you to know how much I enjoyed your work," he said. "Both yours and Miss Langtry's. I assume you share the work equally?"

Bo told him that was right.

"Well, you do it very well indeed. I haven't enjoyed any-thing quite so much since the first Ellery Queen novel I ever read. *The Roman Hat Mystery*, I believe. And to think that both you and Miss Langtry live right here in the city! I wonder if you would do me the honor of having dinner with me some evening?"

Ray had gotten their names from an article that appeared in the local newspaper after the publication of *The Red and Blue Clue*. No other newspapers had been interested, which was fine with Bo. He thought writers should write and not have to worry about publicizing their work.

The young reporter who came to do the interview had been struck by the fact that the book was a collaboration between a man and a woman, and he'd written a long story about how the two had met (at the library), discovered their mutual interest in mysteries (they were in the mystery section and both of them reached at the same time for the latest John Dickson Carr novel), and decided to write together (both had friends who said things like "You read so many of those things, why don't you write one?" but neither felt competent to try it alone).

Ray Thompson loved reading, especially mysteries, and he had time to indulge himself thanks to his enviable financial situation. His father had bought a few acres of land to raise cows on and had forgotten all about the cows when a drilling company discovered oil there. He retired from raising cattle and doing much of anything except counting his money, and Ray had followed in the old man's footsteps, except that now most of the oil was gone and the money came in from investments.

Janice and Bo had gone to dinner at Ray's house a few days after the phone call. Neither had ever been in a place quite like it. When they entered the front door, they were only a few steps from the largest private library in the city with wooden bookshelves filled from floor to ceiling with nothing but mystery novels, first editions by Agatha Christie, Ngaio Marsh, Ellery Queen, Dorothy L. Sayers, Cornell Woolrich (and his alter ego William Irish), John Dickson Carr (and *his* alter ego, Carter Dickson), and even (to Bo's secret delight) Mickey Spillane.

Ray was as fascinated with the two writers as they were with his books. For all his love of reading, he had never met an actual writer before, and now he was talking to two of them. After that evening they were fast friends, and Janice and Bo were frequent guests in Ray's home. But now he was dead.

"I just can't believe it," Janice said as Bo pulled to the curb in front of Ray's house.

There were several cars already there: two police cars, Lt. Franklin's unmarked Ford, and a black Lincoln Continental.

The two-story house was huge and impressive, if not exactly tasteful, with a wide front and two wings that extended backward. The outside was mostly red brick, and there were flowerbeds along the front and down the sidewalk.

"I'm not sure I want to go in there," Janice said.

Bo wasn't so sure either. He was used to murder on the clean white pages he typed, but he had never been on the scene of an actual killing.

"We have to go in," he said.

He got out of the car and went around to open the passenger door for Janice. It was still raining lightly, and the December wind moaned out of the gray sky and whipped down the street, cutting right through Bo's red jacket. Janice was wearing a long all-weather coat with a raccoon collar. The bottom of it flapped against her legs as she stepped out on the curb.

There were two tall oak trees in the front yard of the house. The wind scattered dead, wet leaves across the yard and down the sidewalk, and they brushed across Bo's shoes as he approached the door.

The door was made of heavy carved wood, and there were long windows on either side of it. On the wall beside the windows there were drainpipes coming down from the roof gutters. The water from the drains flowed into the flowerbeds. There was a steady stream from one pipe, but only a trickle from the other.

In the center of the door there was a heavy brass knocker in the shape of a cowboy boot. Bo reached out for the knocker, but he didn't have to use it. The door was pulled open by Lt. Franklin, who was standing in the short hallway. Franklin had a broad face with a down-turned mouth, a nose like a potato, and the suspicious eyes of the career cop.

"C'mon in," he said. His voice was deep and husky, as if he had a terrible cold, which he didn't. He sounded like that all the time.

Bo and Janice walked past him, and he shut the door behind them. Bo helped Janice off with her coat, getting another good whiff of White Shoulders, and hung it in the hall closet. There was already a topcoat inside. The shoulders were slightly damp with rain. The coat looked expensive to Bo, but he wasn't really much of a judge.

It was only a couple of steps from the hall to the library, which looked pretty much as it always had except for the two cops who were going over it as if looking for clues. The major crime scene investigation had already been done, and there was fingerprint powder on every smooth surface that Bo could see. One of the cops was poking through the drawers of the desk. The other was taking books off the shelves and thumbing through the pages.

The library was a large room, about fifteen feet wide by twenty feet long, with most of the available wall space being taken up by the bookshelves. There was, however, a large stone fireplace on the wall at the right end of the room. Opposite the room's entrance there was a big oak desk, and behind the desk were French doors leading onto a stone patio and into the yard beyond. Bo noticed that one of the doors had a broken pane.

"That's where it happened," Franklin said, waving a hand toward the library. "The body was right there by the desk."

"You said he was shot, didn't you?" Janice asked.

Franklin nodded.

"What about the gun, then?"

"She means the murder weapon," Bo said, trying to show Franklin that they knew the jargon.

Franklin wasn't interested in jargon, however. He obviously had something else on his mind.

"The gun's one of our problems," he said.

"You said you couldn't find it," Janice prompted.

"That's right. Listen, why don't you two come in the library with me for a minute?"

Franklin moved away without waiting for an answer. Bo looked at Janice, who nodded, and the two of them followed the police lieutenant.

Franklin stopped just inside the library. "Let's not get in anybody's way," he said.

The two cops went about their business. The one looking through the books put the one he had been examining back on the shelf and took another one down. The other cop was finished with the desk drawers, and he moved to another part of the room and began examining books just as his partner was doing.

Bo noticed the floor beside the desk. There was a large dark stain in the carpet.

"Why did you want us to come in here?" Bo asked, trying not to look at the stain.

"Because there are some other people being interviewed in

the den," Franklin said. "I've already talked to them, but Simmons is going over things with them again."

Simmons was a homicide detective. Bo and Janice had talked to him a few times when he dropped by Franklin's office while they were visiting.

"We couldn't talk in here," Franklin went on, with a glance at the stain that Bo was trying to ignore. "The den was the best place."

The den was in the wing of the house to the left of the library. The downstairs area of that wing also held the game room and a large storage room. The other wing was for the kitchen, the dining room, and the office where Ray took care of his business interests. Bedrooms were upstairs in both wings.

"Why did you want us to come over here, anyway?" Janice asked. "Ray was our friend, but that's not why you called. Is it?"

Franklin looked uncomfortable. "No," he admitted. "That's not why I called."

Janice wasn't satisfied with that. "So why *did* you call, then?"

"You know how these things are," Franklin said. "Real murder's not like it is in those books you write, or it's not supposed to be."

Bo was getting interested. "What do you mean?"

"I mean, murder's usually something that's pretty straightforward. You have witnesses. You have clues. You have people who know things."

"But not this time?"

"Not this time. This time it *is* like one of your books."

"Tell us about it," Janice said.

3

Franklin told them what he knew. The missing gun was the least of his problems. What he had was a locked-room crime.

"Hank Rollins heard the shots," the lieutenant said. "He's sort of an all 'round handyman that Thompson used for all kinds of work around the place. In the summer he mows the yard, and he makes general repairs when they're needed. This morning he was out in the back, cutting some dead limbs out of the pecan trees when he heard what he thought were two pistol shots. They were muffled, as if they'd come from the house, so Rollins ran to the patio and looked in through the French doors."

"Thompson was lying on the floor," Franklin said. "There was no one else in the room. Rollins couldn't get in because the French doors were locked. He broke out one of the door panes and came inside. When he got in, he could hear someone banging on the front door knocker. He looked down at Thompson, figured he needed help, and went to the door. There was a guy named Walton standing there."

"Jeffery Walton?" Janice asked.

Franklin nodded. "That's right. You know him?"

Bo had heard the name. "Ray's business manager. Ray's talked about him to us. We've never met him."

"Well, he was the guy at the door. He and Rollins went back to the library, and the daughter was there by that time, standing by the body and screaming. Walton took her out of the room, and Rollins called us."

"They didn't see the gun?" Janice asked.

"They didn't see anything," Franklin said. "So they say. But there were some other people here."

"Who?" Bo wanted to know.

"Thompson's kids."

"Dolly and Jimmy," Janice said. "Them, we've met."

"They're the ones. The girl was upstairs in what she calls her 'sewing room.' "

"Sewing's her hobby," Janice said. "She's very good."

Franklin didn't look as if he cared a thing about Dolly's sewing skills. "Yeah. Anyway, the room's right by her bedroom, and she was making a dress or something, running a little Singer machine. She says she heard the shots, but they were muffled, like someone hitting a nail with a hammer. She didn't know what they were. She left the sewing room to check, and then she heard the glass break. She got downstairs just about the time Rollins was letting Walton in the front door."

"Did anyone hear the door knocker before the shots?" Janice asked.

"That's an interesting question," Franklin said. "And the answer is no, and as far as anyone knows, there was no one in the house except Thompson."

"What about Jimmy?" Bo asked.

"He didn't hear the door knocker or the shots, he says. Says he was in the garage, working on his car."

The garage was separate from the house, just in back. There was a door that led from the kitchen to a short covered walk that went to the garage.

"He likes that car, all right," Bo said. "It's a '55 Chevy Bel-Air with a V-8 engine and—"

"I don't care about the damn car," Franklin said. "Don't you see what we've got here?"

"I do," Janice said. "It's like something from one of our books. A man was murdered in this room, by someone that no one knows was in the house. The victim had a door behind him and a door in front of him, but it seems that the killer didn't go out either of them. He didn't go out the back door, or Jimmy would've seen him from the garage. And he didn't go upstairs to the bedrooms on Dolly's side, because she didn't see him there."

"What about the den?" Bo asked. "Aren't there French doors in there, too?"

"Bolted," Franklin said. "On the inside."

"Then the killer's still in the house," Bo said.

"He's not in the house," Franklin told him. "You can bet on that. We've searched."

Bo looked over at the fireplace. There hadn't been a fire in it in a long time; Ray thought the smoke wasn't good for his books. There seemed to Bo to be an excess of soot on the hearth, however, as if someone had disturbed the interior of the chimney. Bo had no idea how big the chimney was, but it was certainly possible that someone could have climbed up it. Chimney sweeps did it in seventeenth-century London, though of course they were mostly small children.

Of course Dr. Gideon Fell, one of John Dickson Carr's famous fictional detectives, didn't approve of chimneys as a means of escape in locked-room murders, but maybe Thompson's killer didn't know that.

"If the killer's not in the house, and if no one saw him making his escape, where does that leave you?" Janice asked Franklin.

"I don't know," he said. "That's why I called you two. Most murders are really pretty simple. There's not any puzzle to figure out. You just look for motive, means, and opportunity, and when you've got all that sorted out, you can find your killer."

"Speaking of motives, you have a couple of people here who have one," Bo said. Janice glared at him, but he went on.

"Let's face it. We liked Ray, but Dolly and Jimmy didn't get along with their father."

"The kids," Franklin said. "We know about that, too."

It was an old and familiar story. The mother dies when the children are young, and the father tries to compensate by being overly strict, possibly a bit dictatorial.

Ray Thompson had wanted Jimmy, the eldest, to make his own way in the world, while Jimmy had become more than a little resentful when he did not receive the help he expected. Jimmy had managed well enough, however. He worked his way through college and law school, and he was now living at home while studying for the bar exam. His one luxury was the '55 Chevy that Ray had recently bought him. Ray had told Bo and Janice that he was getting older and that it was time he started loosening the purse strings.

Dolly was twenty, five years younger than her brother, and not nearly so resentful, though it was no real secret that she felt a bit ridiculous wearing homemade clothes while most of the girls from other families she knew were wearing fashion originals.

"She's been known to comment that she wouldn't mind getting her hands on her inheritance," Franklin said.

"How could you possibly know that?" Janice asked.

Franklin smiled as much as it was possible for him to do so. "You don't think I move in the right social circles?"

"She just wondered who told you," Bo said, though he could guess. It had to have been either Jimmy Thompson or Jeffery Walton. "What do you know about Hank Rollins?"

"Glad you asked," Franklin said. "There's no police file on him, not even a parking ticket. He's worked for Thompson for years, mowing the yard, painting, things like that. And he's done odd jobs for a lot of people in the neighborhood. There's never been a complaint."

81

"Sometimes it's the one you least suspect," Bo said.

"Could be," Franklin said. "Maybe he thought there was some money in the desk. But then why would he answer the front door?"

"What about Walton?" Bo asked.

"Well, now," Franklin said. "He doesn't have a record, either. But he and Thompson haven't exactly been getting along lately, and Walton came here with some bad news."

"What bad news?" Janice asked.

"It seems that nearly all Thompson's investments have gone south on him. Walton was going to tell him that he was practically broke."

"That might give *Ray* a motive for murder," Janice said. "If he blamed Walton. But it wouldn't give Walton a reason for killing Ray."

"I'm just telling you what I know," Franklin said. "Maybe none of them did it. Maybe Thompson was killed by the Invisible Man, who just walked out the front door without being seen."

"I didn't notice Claude Rains walking the streets on the way over here," Bo said.

"I didn't ask you here to make jokes," Franklin said. "I thought maybe you'd have some ideas."

"We do," Janice said, surprising Bo, who had no ideas at all. "Can we talk to everyone?"

"Together?" Franklin asked.

"No. One at a time."

"Sure. I'll arrange it. In the den be OK?"

"The kitchen," Janice said. "I want to talk to Bo in there first, alone."

"You two go ahead," Franklin said. "I'll get things set up."

Janice thanked him and started for the kitchen. Bo

watched her go. She turned back. "Are you coming?"

"I guess so," Bo said, still wondering what she knew that he didn't.

4

As soon as they got into the kitchen, Bo lit up a Camel. He looked around for an ashtray, but there wasn't one. He tossed the match in the sink.

"That's a disgusting thing to do," Janice said. "I suppose you're going to put your ashes there, too."

"That's right," Bo said. "It may be disgusting, but it's safer than flicking them in the trash can. Don't worry. I'll wash out the sink when I'm done."

Janice started out of the kitchen. "I'm sure you will."

"Hey, where're you going?"

"To look at something. You just smoke your cigarette. I'll be right back."

Bo inhaled deeply and let the smoke trickle out through his nose. *Fills your lungs with tiny little vitamins,* he thought. He looked around the kitchen. Ray had a housekeeper, but maybe today was her day off. She kept the place excessively clean, in Bo's opinion. The countertops sparkled, and the porcelain sink was so white that it hurt his eyes to look at it. All of which led him to wonder again about the chimney and all that soot.

He was thinking about that when Janice came back into the room.

She looked pointedly at the cigarette. "Aren't you finished yet?"

Bo was only about halfway down the Camel, but he stuck it under the tap and turned on the water. The cigarette fizzed and went out. He dropped it in the sink.

"I'll get it," he said. "I promise."

"You'd better. Now, what do you think about all this?"

"It's obvious," Bo said. "The chimney. Did you notice all the soot on the hearth? I think someone killed Ray and escaped up the chimney. That's the only way it could've been done."

"Assuming someone could actually climb up the chimney," Janice said, "which I doubt, where did he go after that?"

"The roof," Bo said.

"And then?"

"Down a drainpipe maybe. There're two of them right by the front door."

"Wouldn't he have been seen?"

"Maybe there's a drainpipe in the back," Bo said, getting into the spirit of it. "Here's how I'd plot it. The killer comes in, argues with Ray for some reason or another. Then something gets Ray really upset and he goes for that pistol he keeps in his desk—"

Bo broke off and looked at Janice. "The pistol! Ray showed it to us one night. It's in the middle drawer of the desk! I've got to tell Franklin."

He started for the doorway, but Janice stopped him. "The pistol's not there. I looked."

"So that's where you went. Did you tell anyone?"

Janice shook her head. The ponytail jiggled. "I mentioned it to Lt. Franklin."

"Good. What did he say?"

"He said they'd look for it."

"All right. Anyway, it all fits. Ray goes for the pistol. They struggle, and the killer takes the gun away from him. Ray charges, the killer fires. Ray drops, and the killer is horrified by what he's done. How can he escape? His eyes dart around

84

the room. Suddenly, he hears the knocking on the front door! He sees Rollins coming toward the patio from the back yard! Maybe he even hears Dolly coming down the stairs!"

Bo was half-crouched in the middle of the kitchen now, his palms held outward at shoulder level. He was taking the part of the killer, and his head swiveled from right to left as he searched desperately for an exit.

"Where can he go? There's no way out! But then he sees the chimney! Can he get inside?"

Bo glided across the kitchen toward the Chambers range. He opened the oven door and looked inside.

"It looks awfully small, but he has to try! It's his only chance!"

"You're not really going to try to get in there, are you?" Janice asked, as Bo stuck his head inside the oven.

Bo pulled his head back and grinned sheepishly. "Sorry. I guess I got a little carried away. But you see how it would work, don't you?"

"Maybe," Janice said, but she didn't look convinced.

"Just think of it," Bo told her. "Close your eyes and imagine it. He scrabbles up the chimney and comes out on the roof, covered in black soot. The wind is howling around him—"

"The wind is a little gusty," Janice said, "but it isn't howlin'."

"Hey," Bo said, "we're working on a story here. Give me a little poetic license."

"All right," Janice said. "Go on. 'The wind is howlin' around him—' "

"Right. It's dark, and the moon is hiding behind the thick clouds—"

"Dark? It's overcast, but it's not dark."

"It is in the story, all right?"

"Fine. It's your story."

"Damn right. Do you want to hear the rest of it?"

"Of course. But why don't we talk to people first? They might give you some ideas."

Bo could see the sense in that, though he hated to stop when he was going so well. Nevertheless, he said, "You're right. Are you ready?"

"I think so. Would you like to talk to Dolly first?"

"Why not? You want me to have Franklin send her in?"

"Go ahead."

5

Dolly was tall and slender, with black hair, black eyes, and pale skin. Her eyes were red now, as if she had been crying. She was sitting at the sturdy oak kitchen table across from Janice. Bo was sitting at the end, in the only chair with arms.

Dolly explained that after hearing the shots, though she didn't know at the time what they were, she thought she had better see if something had happened in the lower part of the house.

"It was such an *unusual* noise," she said. "And when I got downstairs, there was Father, lying on the rug."

Her voice broke, and she looked down at the tabletop. Janice reached across the table to take her hand. "Let's not talk about that part. Tell me about what you heard before the shots."

Dolly looked up. "Before the shots?"

"Yes," Janice said. "Did you hear anything? The door knocker? Anything at all?"

"Mr. Franklin asked me that," Dolly said. "I told him no. I didn't hear a thing."

"Think hard," Janice said, and Bo wondered what she was getting at. "Close your eyes and try to imagine that you're back in your room. You're sewing, and the house is quiet. Can you hear anything at all?"

For a full minute Dolly said nothing. Then she said, "Maybe I can hear voices. But not loud. It's hard to hear things up there on the second floor."

"What kind of voices?" Janice asked.

"Angry maybe," Dolly said. "I'm just not sure."

Bo was sure. And he was elated. It was just exactly as he'd thought. An argument. Could he plot, or could he plot?

Dolly left the kitchen and Jimmy came in. Though he had just completed his law degree, he looked more like a mechanic than an attorney. He was wearing overalls with black grease stains on them and a blue work shirt that looked even worse than the overalls. There was even a smear of grease on his face.

Jimmy told them even less than Dolly had. From the garage he could hear nothing at all.

"Were the garage doors open?" Janice asked.

Jimmy told her that they weren't. "Too windy," he explained.

Bo didn't know the point of that exchange, either. What difference did it make whether the garage doors were open? But he didn't worry about it. He had everything figured now. He pictured the killer climbing carefully down the drainpipe, then slipping quietly away through the dripping pecan trees in back of the house.

Jimmy couldn't tell them anything else. "I wish I'd heard someone," he said. "Maybe I could have done something."

Bo didn't think he really seemed all that concerned.

"Or maybe you would have been shot, too," Janice said.

"Maybe," Jimmy said, and then he left the room.

Jeffery Walton was next. He came in with his hand out and a smile like a used car salesman. He was wearing a light gray wool suit that Bo figured had set him back about three Sam Fernando royalty statements. There was a dark stain on one knee of the suit.

"I'm Ray's business manager," Walton said. "He often told me about you two. I'm sorry we have to meet under these circumstances."

Bo shook Walton's hand. "It's not your fault."

"How long have you been associated with Ray?" Janice asked.

Walton thought for a moment. "Fifteen years, give or take a few months. We did a lot of business together."

"But things haven't gone so well lately, have they?" Janice asked.

Walton lost his smile. "That's correct. The market hasn't behaved as a lot of us thought it would."

Bo didn't know a thing about that, and he didn't think Janice did, either. Neither of them had any money in the market, though the Gentleman Sleuth books were beginning to pay off. Bo had a fairly sizeable savings account, and it was time he started thinking of other kinds of investments.

"I don't suppose Ray was happy about that," Janice said.

"Neither was I," Walton told her.

"Is that your camel's hair coat in the hall closet?" Janice asked. "It's very nice."

"Yes," Walton said. "It's mine. I'm glad you like it."

"Can you think of anyone who might have wanted Ray dead?" Bo asked. He was tired of all the irrelevant questions Janice was asking everyone.

"Several people," Walton said. He looked over his shoulder toward the other part of the house. "I don't want to talk about anyone, but—"

"Never mind," Janice said. "We know that Ray wasn't on the best of terms with his children."

"I meant anyone outside the family," Bo said.

"I really can't think of anyone," Walton admitted. "Ray was on pretty good terms with everyone."

He gave it some more thought at Bo's urging, but he still couldn't come up with any names, so Janice asked if there were any cars in the street when he drove up.

"I didn't see any."

Bo didn't see the point of that one. He started to say so, but Janice was already asking Walton to send in Hank Rollins.

Rollins was tall and slender, with a weathered face and hands. He was wearing a flannel shirt, a denim jacket, and faded jeans. Janice asked him to tell what had happened earlier.

"I heard the shots," Rollins said, his voice quivering slightly. "Two of 'em. I got to the house quick as I could, but I was cuttin' some dead limbs out of those pecan trees in back, and it took me a second or two to get movin'. I looked in through those funny doors, and I could see Mr. Ray was lyin' right there on the floor."

"And there was no one else in the room?" Janice said.

"Not a single, solitary soul. I broke out one of them little glass panes and opened the doors. I seen right off there wasn't a thing I could do."

"And there was someone knocking at the front door?" Janice asked.

"Yep. It was that Mr. Walton. I let him in, and by that time Miss Dolly was in the library. She seen her daddy lyin' there and busted out screamin'. Mr. Walton took her in the den to try calmin' her down, and I called the cops."

"Did you see any cars on the street when you opened the door?" Janice asked.

89

"Nope. Just that big Lincoln that Mr. Walton drives."

Bo finally figured out why Janice had asked Jimmy about the garage doors. She wanted to know if he could see the street. But he still didn't see why she wanted to know. By the time he'd thought about it for a few seconds, Janice was asking Rollins exactly what Walton did when he went into the library.

"Well, that's hard to say. Miss Dolly was standin' there, and Walton got down on his knees to see if Mr. Ray was dead."

The dark stain on the knee of the suit was blood, Bo thought.

"I hope he didn't get any blood on that expensive top coat," Janice said.

"Oh, he wasn't wearin' any coat," Rollins told her.

Bo wondered about the man who'd gone up the chimney. He ought to be easy to spot. His coat and pants would have soot all over them. He hoped the police were doing a search of the neighborhood.

Janice was through with Rollins. He left the room, his shoulders slumped as if he were carrying something heavy. He looked as if he was the only one who was really sad about Ray Thompson's death.

"Are you finished talking to them?" Bo asked.

"I think so. Are you ready to play Sam Fernando?"

"Huh? What are you talking about?"

"I'm talking about calling all the suspects together in the den and pulling the killer out of a hat."

"That's a mixed metaphor," Bo said. "At least I think it is. I figured you for a better writer than that."

"You know what I mean. Are you ready?"

"You mean you're not kidding? Do have any idea what you're talking about?"

Janice smiled. "Of course I do. Don't you?"

"The chimney," Bo said. "It has to be the chimney."

"Don't be silly. All that soot? The police must've caused that when they searched it. You don't think they'd miss somethin' that obvious, do you?"

"Rats," Bo said. "Probably not."

"And if the killer kicked out the soot, wouldn't Mr. Rollins or Mr. Walton or Dolly have noticed it fallin' out of the chimney? Wouldn't they have heard him scrabblin' around in there?"

"I guess so," Bo said. He was quite disappointed. It had all seemed so logical.

"You get it now, though, don't you?" Janice asked.

Bo had to admit that he didn't, so Janice told him.

6

Jimmy Thompson sat uncomfortably in an overstuffed leather-covered chair that looked as if it belonged in a lawyer's office instead of a den. Jeffery Walton and Dolly sat on a long floral-covered couch. Hank Rollins sat in a wingback chair. Franklin, Bo, and Janice stood near the center of the room. Detective Simmons was standing at one end of the couch. It was time for the big moment.

Franklin had everyone's attention as he began speaking. "As you all know, Miss Langtry and Mr. Wagner are more or less experts in unusual murder cases like this, and they were also friends of the victim. I asked them to come over and give us the benefit of their expertise, and they tell me they know who killed Mr. Thompson."

Everyone looked a little shocked at that bit of news, and Jimmy Thompson leaned forward. "Are you joking? They're just writers, not trained investigators. They don't know anything about real life."

Bo had never particularly disliked Jimmy before, but now he saw that, given the opportunity, he could develop quite an antipathy to the young man.

"They may be writers, but they do know something about locked rooms. Mr. Wagner?"

Bo straightened and tried to look dignified in the Sam Fernando manner, but it wasn't easy while wearing a green shirt and a red jacket with jeans that had a hole in the knee. Sam Fernando wouldn't have been caught dead in any such get-up. Bo thought Janice would have been much more impressive in the role, but she wanted him to do it.

"When you have a murder like this," Bo said, "you have to consider the usual things: motive, means, and opportunity. The problem with this particular case is that there doesn't seem to have *been* an opportunity." He paused dramatically, just as Sam Fernando often did. "But there was."

"Baloney," Jimmy said. "There was no one in the room when Rollins came in, and my father was dead."

"But there was someone in the room," Bo said. "Or there had been."

Jimmy was still belligerent. "So how did he get in? Dolly didn't ever hear the knocker. Neither did I."

"You tell 'em, Janice," Bo said. He wanted her to get some of the glory. After all, it was her idea. Besides, she could take some of the blame if it all turned out to be wrong.

"No one heard the knocker because no one used it," Janice said. "We didn't use it when we came. Lt. Franklin was waiting at the door for us, and he saw us coming through the glass panes on either side. Ray was waiting for someone he badly wanted to see. When that person arrived, Ray was at the door and opened it for him."

"And who was that person?" Walton asked.

"You should know," Bo said. "It was you."

Walton half rose from the couch. "That's ridiculous."

"No it isn't," Bo said. "Ray let you in. I think he suspected that you'd been jiggling his accounts. He told me and Janice that he was thinking about letting Jimmy and Dolly have a little more money, and I figure that when he discussed that with you, you told him that it wasn't available. He wanted to know why. Maybe you stalled him for a while, but you couldn't put him off forever. He demanded a face-to-face meeting. There was an argument. Maybe you threatened him. He went for the pistol he kept in his desk. You took it away from him, and then you shot him."

Walton was breathing hard. "Utterly ridiculous. You can't prove a word of it."

"There were no other cars on the street," Bo went on. "Therefore the killer either walked here—unlikely in this weather—or drove. Only one person drove."

"He could have been here already," Walton pointed out. He was getting his breathing back under control. "What about Dolly and Jimmy? What about Rollins?"

"I guess it could be one of them," Bo said. "But it wasn't. Tell him what gave him away, Janice."

"That topcoat you said was yours," she told Walton. "It's hanging in the closet. You took it off when you came in the first time, and you didn't have time to put it back on. Maybe you didn't even think about it, but you were mighty calm if you ask me. Calm enough to know that if you hurried, you could get back outside before anybody got here to investigate the shots. Then you could bang on the door and pretend you were just arrivin'. But Mr. Rollins will swear that you didn't have the coat on when he let you in. Won't you, Mr. Rollins?"

"I sure as to God will," Rollins said. He looked as if he

would like to come out of the wingback chair and throttle Walton right there in the library.

"You still can't prove I killed him," Walton said. "There's no weapon."

"Not right now," Bo said. "But it couldn't be far. In fact, I'd bet it's jammed up the drain spout right out there by the front door."

That was when Walton jumped for him.

Bo squared off and raised his fists, much as he imagined Mike Hammer would have done in a similar situation, but he didn't get to test his talent for violence. Detective Simmons put a big hand on Walton's collar and jerked him back down on the couch.

"There, there," Simmons said. "None of that."

Walton snorted and tried to twist out of Simmons' grip, but he couldn't. He sat and stared balefully at Bo and Janice.

Dolly was looking at Walton strangely. "I don't understand," she said. "Why didn't he just get in his car and leave?"

"He was probably afraid someone would see him," Bo said, though he wasn't sure about that part. Janice hadn't told him what she thought.

Now, however, she did. "It was probably because he was afraid someone here would know that he had an appointment with Dad today. I don't think anyone did, but what if Ray had written it on his calendar? Walton could have justified being late, but he might not have been able to explain things if he didn't show up at all."

Franklin called the two policemen who had been in the library earlier and told one of them to check the drainpipe. The man was back in less than a minute.

"It's in there, all right. I didn't want to touch it."

"We'll get it later," Franklin said. "It's not going anywhere, and those fingerprints won't wash off so easily. Take

Mr. Walton to the station, boys."

"With pleasure," Simmons said, jerking Walton up off the couch.

Walton tried to say something, but his voice was too choked by Simmons' grip on his collar to be intelligible. Bo figured that was just as well.

7

While they were driving back to the house to finish work on their book, Bo sulked behind the wheel.

After they had gone a few blocks, Janice said, "You don't seem too happy that we cracked the case."

Bo stared out moodily through the windshield. It was no longer raining, but the sky was still heavy with clouds. The radio was playing "Walking Along" by the Diamonds, a number that would normally have cheered him up. But not this time.

"I didn't crack anything. You did."

"What difference does that make? We made sure that Ray's killer didn't get away with it."

Bo turned his head to look at her. "I didn't make sure. I thought all the time that it was the chimney." He faced front again.

"That doesn't matter. You were looking at it like a story. I was looking at it like real life. Besides, we're a team. Partners. I learned everything I know about figuring out plots from reading your outlines. Even if the spelling is atrocious."

"Really? You mean that?"

"Sure I do. I couldn't have figured it out without knowing the way you think about things."

"Maybe you don't need me anymore, then."

"Now you know better than that. Didn't I say we were a team? Just like Crosby and Hope."

"Right! Ruth and Gehrig."

"Martin and Lewis."

"They broke up."

"Well, we won't. Just like Burns and Allen."

Bo laughed. "Abbott and Costello."

"Frick and Frack," Janice said, joining in his laughter.

"Damon and Pythias."

"Aeneas and Achates."

"Sodom and Gomorrah," Bo added, hopefully.

"Forget it, bub!"

But Bo thought about it all the way home.

I've always enjoyed writing about English teacher Carl Burns and his friendly adversary "Boss" Napier. They've appeared in three books and two Christmas stories.

The Santa Claus Caper

"Pum-pum-pum-pum-*puuum*-pum—pum-pum-pum-pum-pum."

R. M. "Boss" Napier, chief of the Pecan City, Texas, police, puffed his cheeks and pummed the words to the theme from his favorite TV show, *Hawaii Five-O*. Still available every evening, thanks to cable. He accompanied himself by patting his hands on the edge of his battered wooden desk.

Thinking of white sand beaches, blue skies and bluer waves, he resolutely resisted turning to look out the window at his back. Had he done so, he would have seen that the dark sky in the north was getting darker still, turning a deep blue that was almost black as the norther that was sweeping down on Pecan City got closer and closer.

It wasn't so much that Napier disliked the wind and the cold that he knew was coming. After all, you expected that kind of weather in West Texas in December.

What he disliked was that it was almost Christmas, a time of year which did not generally make him a more kindly and benevolent person.

As far as he was concerned, it didn't make anybody more kindly and benevolent. What it did was bring out the shoplifters and the burglars, increase the number of assaults and accidents involving drunken drivers, and generally wreak havoc with the community.

And worse even than those things, Napier had somehow let himself be talked into taking part in a community activity.

He didn't like community activities, but he'd let himself be persuaded by Carl Burns, that wimp English teacher out at the college, to be part of something Burns called a "readers' theater" version of "A Christmas Carol."

"You'll love it," Burns told him. "And even if you don't, think of all the people who'll come and bring their kids. Think of all those potential voters."

It was something to think about, all right. In Pecan City, the office of police chief was elective rather than appointed.

"Besides," Burns said, "the Mayor will be reading a part. So will I. It's sort of like your civic duty."

Napier thought he was doing his civic duty by serving as police chief. He didn't see why he had to be in some ridiculous play.

"It's not ridiculous," Burns said. "Just think of it as a favor to me. I've helped you out a time or two."

Napier didn't like to admit it, but Burns had a point. The English teacher wasn't really such a wimp, and he'd been in on two murder cases that might not have gotten solved without him, or at least not solved as quickly as they had been.

"I don't like to read," Napier said. "Not out loud, anyway."

"It's easy," Burns said. "Miss Tanner will be reading, too."

Well, that was different. Elaine Tanner was the librarian at the college, and Napier liked her a lot. Her blonde hair, her green eyes . . .

"So how about it?" Burns said.

"OK, I'll do it. What part do I get?"

"Well, we might all be reading more than one, but you'll have at least one major role."

"OK. What major role?"

"It'll be a good one. Don't worry."

"Yeah, I'm sure. But you better tell me what it is."

Burns smiled. "Tiny Tim," he said.

Napier had not killed Burns on the spot, though he'd thought about it. No jury in the world would have convicted him. After all, he was the Chief, and he could tell everyone that Burns had been killed while attempting to escape. It might have worked, as long as no one pointed out that Burns hadn't been a prisoner and therefore had no reason to attempt escape.

Anyway, much to Napier's surprise things had worked out all right. Tiny Tim really was a good part, and Napier had a reading voice that carried well, even if it was a little deep and resonant for a kid like Tiny Tim. Napier refused to do the part in falsetto, though Burns had asked him to give it a try.

The best part about the whole thing was that Elaine Tanner was impressed by Napier's abilities, a fact that irritated Burns no end.

"You really are good at this, R.M.," she said after the first rehearsal. She was standing close to him, with her hand resting lightly on his arm. "Are you sure you've never been on the stage before?"

Napier had to admit that he hadn't. His only stage experience had been in the first grade, when he'd portrayed a woodpecker in some stupid play about where birds go in the winter. He'd had to stand on a chair behind a fake cedar tree.

"He's a natural," Burns said, walking over to join them. "I think he practices by intimidating criminals."

"Well, he's really very good," Elaine said. "No matter how he got that way."

Napier smiled at her, and he smiled even more when he

saw how much Elaine's comment rankled Burns. The two men had been dating the librarian since the beginning of the school year in September, but neither one of them had gained an advantage to this point. Napier thought maybe he was gaining now.

So Napier really didn't mind leaving his office at the city jail for the rehearsal to be held in the college auditorium. He'd be seeing Elaine again, and he'd get yet another chance to provoke Burns. He didn't want to provoke him too much, though. He had something he wanted Burns to do for him, something that had to do with the reasons Napier didn't enjoy Christmas.

The norther struck just as Napier left the jail. It kicked up white dust in the parking lot and blew grit in Napier's mouth and eyes. Although it was not quite four o'clock in the afternoon, it was nearly as dark as night. The wind was whipping along at around thirty-five miles an hour, straight from the North Pole, and Napier was sure that the temperature dropped fifteen degrees between the time he left the jail and the time he reached his car. He pulled his leather coat tighter around a waist that seemed a little thicker than he remembered it and thought about surfers flashing across the tops of the blue waves in the opening scenes of *Five-O*. He wondered if they needed any more cops in Honolulu.

"God bless us, every one," Napier said.

Don Elliott, the director, applauded. "Very well done. Very well done, indeed. I especially liked the way you read the part of Scrooge this time, Mayor Riley. Just the right amount of menace." Elliott was short, hardly more than five feet, but his voice was even more impressive than Napier's. It could be heard all over the auditorium.

Mayor Riley smirked at Elliott's compliment. Riley was a

100

lawyer, and he fancied that he knew a thing or two about menace.

"Professor Burns, you need to do a bit more cringing as Cratchit, at least at first. You can't let the audience off the hook too easily," Elliott said.

This time it was Napier who smirked, but not for long. He didn't want to alienate Burns just now. After Elliott was through with his comments, Napier walked over to where Burns was talking to Elaine Tanner. Napier thought again how much he liked the way Elaine's glasses magnified her green eyes.

"Sorry," Burns said when Napier reached them. "No time to talk this evening. Elaine and I are going out for a bite to eat."

"Why don't you come with us, R.M.?" Elaine said. "Unless you have some important police business to attend to?"

Napier smiled, not so much at the invitation as at a noise he was sure must be Burns' teeth grinding.

"Thanks," he said. "I need to talk to Burns, anyhow. This'll give me a chance."

"Talk to me?" Burns said. "What about?"

"I'll tell you while we eat," Napier said. "Why don't we go to the Taco Bell?"

There weren't many good restaurants in Pecan City, but Burns plainly had somewhere a little fancier in mind. He started to say something, but Napier beat him to it. "My treat."

"Well," Burns said, "since you put it that way, how can I refuse?"

"You can't. Why don't I take Elaine with me? She can ride in the squad car."

"Oh, can I?" Elaine's eyes sparkled. She loved police talk, and she loved to ride in official vehicles.

"Sure," Napier said. "Meet you there, Burns?"

"Fine," Burns said, his teeth grinding as he watched them walk away.

The wind lashed the green plastic wreaths attached to the utility poles and tore at the red, green, and white Christmas lights strung in the trees. It shook Carl Burns' old green Plymouth as Burns drove toward the Taco Bell. Burns looked out at the decorations and tried to relax his jaws, though what he saw didn't help much.

Lawns and rooftops were covered with the usual floodlit Santas and reindeer, shepherds, Wise Men, and babes in mangers. The wind had bowled over some of the figures, and they lay face down on stiff brown grass. On one lawn there was a parade of the characters from the Peanuts comic strip, except for Snoopy. Where the dancing beagle should have been there was a black and white sign that said

SNOOPY STOLEN FROM THIS SPOT 12/24/89.

And where was the Pecan City Police Force when that crime was being committed? Burns wondered. Probably scarfing fajitas at the Taco Bell.

When Burns pulled into the parking lot, the squad car was already there. Elaine and Napier were inside, sitting at a table, and Elaine was laughing at something that Napier had said. Burns punished his dental work some more. Who would ever have guessed that Boss Napier could be so smooth?

Napier got up when Burns entered, asked what he was having, and ordered for everyone. The food was ready quickly, and while they ate Napier entertained by telling them why he liked *Hawaii Five-O* and why he hated Christmas.

"As a matter of fact," he said to Burns, "that's what I wanted to talk to you about?"

"You want me to make a list for you?" Burns said. He was fond of making lists, and he had one of his own about the Christmas season.

"Nope," Napier said. "I've got a job for you."

"A job?" Burns said. "I've already got a job."

"Sure you do, but not during Christmas. You teachers relax and get this long holiday while the rest of us have to work. So I know you're free. And besides, the way you get paid, you probably need the money."

Burns' first impulse was to tell Napier that Hartley Gorman College paid a very satisfactory wage, but he restrained himself. He didn't want to lie. Besides, he was curious.

"What's the job?" he said.

"I want you to go undercover," Napier said.

"Oh, Carl," Elaine said. "A police job!"

Napier suddenly had the sinking feeling that he'd made a big mistake, but he went on. "That's right. A police job. We're shorthanded, and I think you can handle this."

"I don't know," Burns said, keeping his eyes on Elaine.

"Of course you can," she said. "You've been a big help to R.M. in the past."

"True," Burns said. "I do seem to have a flair for investigative work."

"I wouldn't call it a flair," Napier said.

"He's done very well," Elaine said. She was sitting on Napier's side of the table, but she looked as if she might move over to join Burns at any minute.

"Tell me about the job," Burns said.

"Investigative work may not be the right phrase either," Napier said.

"Just tell me," Burns said.

"Well, you know how I said I'd be Tiny Tim for you?"

"Of course."

"This is sort of the same thing."

Burns looked skeptical. "You want me to be in a play?"

Napier grinned at him. "You might say that. I want you to play Santa Claus."

The beard itched, the red suit was hot, and the boots were too big. The red fur-trimmed cap kept slipping down over his forehead. The stomach padding made him feel like a whale in a red coat, and the wire-rimmed glasses made everything look blurry.

Carl Burns felt like a complete fool.

He was sitting in the big black chair in the middle of Cameron's Department Store. In front of him, the line of little kiddies was forming. In moments, they would be taking their turns sitting in his lap as they confided to him their secret Christmas wishes.

If he'd had any sense at all, he would have choked Boss Napier with a taco shell, but Elaine had been there and she had looked awed at the idea of Burns actually taking part in a police case, so what could he do? He'd agreed, of course.

The problem was a common one. Cameron's was experiencing high losses to shoplifters, higher than usual even for the season, and the management was at a loss. Their own, trained plainclothes shoppers had been unable to detect what was going on. A few minor offenders had been nabbed, but not enough to stem the flow of merchandise that was leaving the store.

Burns' first thought was that the storeowner should invest in a security system like the ones in the big cities, where an alarm went off if you tried to smuggle something past the sensors.

"They're not making enough money to do that," Napier said, which Burns knew was probably true. The store was old and old-fashioned, and most of the locals preferred to shop in Dallas or Ft. Worth or at the Wal-Mart that had recently been built on the edge of town. Once the store had been the pride of the city, but now it was probably losing money eleven months of the year, and for most of the twelfth. It was only around Christmas that Cameron's had crowds inside, and even then the crowds were not as large as they had been only a few years before.

Burns got a short course in shoplifting from a bored young woman who'd seen it all: the false-bottomed-package gambit, the "I-was-wearing-that-watch-when-I-came-in-here" gambit, the one-garment-over-the-limit-in-the-changing-room gambit, the oversized-handbag gambit, the shove-it-in-the-pants-and/or-coat gambit, and several more.

Then the owner himself, Jay Cameron, briefed Burns in the Santa routine. "My father used to play Santa himself, every year," Cameron said. "He seemed to enjoy it." He shook his head. "Not me, thank you."

He was dressed in an expensive suit that Burns suspected was not bought off his own racks, highly polished leather shoes, a blindingly white shirt, and an earth-tone tie that had probably cost about what Burns made in a week. Maybe the store was doing better than Napier thought.

"You've got to know the names of all the reindeer," Cameron said. "And don't forget Rudolph."

"I won't," Burns said. It wasn't Rudolph that worried him. It was the other six. Or was it seven? Eight?

"You can make up elf names," Cameron said. "But I don't think anybody'll ask."

Burns said that he was relieved to know it.

"Lots of kids are scared of Santa," Cameron said. "If they

start screaming, just let 'em scream. Calming them's not your job. That's for the parents."

Burns didn't like hearing that. He hadn't thought about screaming.

"The suit's waterproof," Cameron said. "So that's one less worry."

"Waterproof?"

"Yeah. In case some kid gets excited and wets his pants."

Great, Burns thought.

"And don't forget to be jolly," Cameron said, dismissing him.

Burns was thinking about being jolly while kids wet their pants and screamed at the same time when the first one climbed in his lap and started explaining why he had to have a complete set of Teenage Mutant Ninja Turtles action figures. He didn't even ask about the reindeer.

By the time the third kid had finished, Burns had more or less relaxed. By the time the fifth had demanded a home computer—"IBM compatible, with a VGA monitor"—Burns was beginning to watch the goings on around the store, paying special attention to the jewelry counter, but not neglecting the electronics section. He was positioned so that he had a good view of both, those being the areas from which a great deal of merchandise seemed to be vanishing.

Over the course of the next few hours, Burns didn't notice a thing out of the ordinary. He assured any number of bright-eyed boys and girls that they would be receiving all the outrageously priced gifts they asked for, explained at least seven times how he was able to cover the whole world in a single night ("Those reindeer are *really* fast. Trust me."), and explained to one very upset little girl that the Grinch was purely a literary conceit, whereas Santa was perfectly real, as the evidence of her own eyes should convince her. He wasn't quite sure she got the idea of the conceit, but he thought she got the point. At least she seemed happier when she got down, but that may have been because he had promised her three Madame Alexander dolls under her tree.

During that time, Burns had seen Jay Cameron visit the jewelry department three times, his eagle eyes seeming to X-ray every handbag and purse. The owner also toured Electronics and stared down several grungy teenagers who looked as if their only purpose in life was to steal personal CD players for their girlfriends. But as far as Burns could tell, none of them took a thing.

The best part of the day for Burns was when Elaine Tanner came in and asked if she could sit on Santa's lap. It really pained Burns to have to turn her down.

Napier turned up later in the afternoon, but Burns had nothing to report.

"Keep watching," Napier said. "We know they're here."

"What about the employees?" Burns said. "I think I read somewhere that employees do most of the shoplifting."

"Not here," Napier said. "Cameron practically undresses them before they leave."

Burns was allowed an hour's break for lunch and dinner. He needed the time. After several hours of balancing chubby kids on his knees, he could hardly stand, much less walk. He ate alone in the storeroom in the back of the store, surrounded by cartons and boxes. He didn't mind. The quiet was a relief.

It was after his dinner break, just past eight o'clock, that he spotted his first shoplifter. He was sure of her almost from the minute he saw her. She had a shifty look when she walked by him, tugging her little boy by the hand, and she didn't let the kid talk to Santa. He didn't even ask to do so. Very suspicious.

She spent quite a long time at the jewelry counter, looking at watches, and the clerk had to turn away several times to help other customers. Again, very suspicious.

Then she left without buying a thing.

Burns was convinced that she had taken something, though he hadn't seen what. Now she had to leave the store with it. That was what Napier had told him, anyhow. "Let 'em get out of the store. That constitutes theft. Just notify the security officer, and he'll do the rest."

Of course the security officer was nowhere to be seen. He was probably somewhere with a doughnut and cup of coffee.

When the woman started for the front door, Burns shoved a tow-headed boy off his lap and stood up.

"But Santa," the boy said. "I haven't finished yet."

"Don't worry, Son," Burns said, trying to be jolly. "You'll get everything you want. Trust me."

"But how do you *know* what I want? I didn't have time—"

"Write me a letter," Burns said, jostling past the other kids in the line. The woman was already out the door, and he was afraid she would be in her car and gone before he got there.

She was only half in the car, however, with one foot still planted on the ground, when Burns tapped her on the shoulder.

"Ma'am?" he said. "Excuse me, ma'am." He had no idea what to say next. What did you say to a shoplifter?

"It's Santa, Mom!" the little boy on the other side of her screamed. "It's Santa!"

The woman looked at Burns. "Whatcha want?" she said.

She was big, Burns realized, almost as big as he was, and he was wearing padding.

"I, ah, I think you might have taken something in there."

The woman stared at Burns, then got slowly out of the car. The boy followed her out. He was very excited to see Santa.

"I wanted to talk to you," he said, "but Mom said we didn't have time. I want a pony for Christmas."

"Be quiet, Larry," the woman said. She stared at Burns. "Whaddya mean about me taking something?"

"I, ah, well, if you'd just let me look in your purse, I'm sure we could clear this up," Burns said. He'd decided that she'd slipped whatever she'd taken into her oversized purse. It had to be there.

"You some kinda creep?" the woman said.

The little boy was shocked. "Don't say that, Mom! It's Santa!"

"Santa's ass," the woman said. "It's some kinda creep." She hugged her purse to her ample bosom as if it contained something precious. "He's one o' them creeps that steals a woman's purse from her at Christmas time."

"No, no," Burns said. "You've got the wrong idea. It's just that I've been—"

"Help!" the woman screamed. "Police! Fire! Rape!"

Burns hadn't noticed until then that there were other people in the parking lot. Now it seemed as if the entire population of Pecan City had arrived at just that moment to do a bit of shopping. Curious faces turned to see what was going on, and two people started walking rapidly in Burns' direction. Burns started to sweat, though the temperature couldn't have been much above freezing.

The little boy didn't know what was going on, but he didn't like it. He looked as if he might cry at any second.

"Help!" the woman screamed. "Police!"

Burns looked around, wishing that he had never seen Napier or Elaine Tanner. It was their fault that he was in this mess, though he knew he had been stupid to follow the woman out of the store. He had no idea how to handle the situation, and he should simply have allowed her to leave.

109

He turned back to the woman, intending to apologize and forget the whole incident.

She swung her purse and hit him in the side of the head. The purse was so heavy Burns thought it might have a compact car inside it.

He shook his head, trying to clear it, and the little boy kicked him in the shin. "You leave my mom alone!" he yelled.

Burns bent to look at his shin, and the woman hit him with her purse again, in the back of the head this time. The fur-rimmed cap protected him to some extent, but Burns went down to his knees on the parking lot.

He heard the horrified voice of a little girl. "That woman's killing Santa!"

The voice did not deter the woman. She hit Burns again.

"What's going on here?" Boss Napier said.

Burns had never thought the Chief's voice could sound so good. He stood up, his right hand pushing the cap out of his eyes.

"This creep was trying to take my purse," the woman said.

"He's a bad Santa," her boy said.

"I was just trying to do what you told me," Burns said.

"I didn't tell you to go picking on solid citizens like Mrs. Branton," Napier said. He looked around at the crowd of curious onlookers. "Everything's all right here now, folks. Just a little Christmas misunderstanding."

"That woman tried to kill Santa," the horrified little girl said.

"Santa's fine. Isn't that right, Santa."

Burns rubbed the back of his head. "Yeah," he said. He didn't even try to be jolly. "Santa's just fine."

As the crowd drifted on into the store, many of them pausing to look back over their shoulders, Burns said to Napier, "You know Mrs. Branton?"

"Right, Mrs. Roy Branton and her fine son Larry." He smiled at the boy, who was watching Burns suspiciously. "This has all been a big misunderstanding, Larry. Santa wasn't trying to take your mother's purse."

"Yes he was," Mrs. Branton said.

"No, no," Napier said, much jollier than Burns had ever seen him. "He's working for me. It was just a mistake. Really. It won't happen again."

Mrs. Branton didn't look convinced. "He looks like a creep to me."

Napier got even jollier. "Well, he's not. You can take my word for it. Right, Santa?"

"Right," Burns said, grinding his teeth.

As Napier explained to Burns later in the storeroom while Burns was getting out of the Santa suit, Mrs. Branton was the ex-wife of one of Napier's best officers. She had quite a reputation around town for her fierce temper and for one other thing—her honesty.

"She's the kind of woman who wouldn't tell a lie even when it would be better than the truth," Napier said. "The kid, Larry, found a ten dollar bill on the street one day, and she made him give it to Harve—Harve's her ex—so Harve could turn it in at the station. We kept it for three weeks, and when no one claimed it, she let Larry have it. She wouldn't steal anything, Burns. She wouldn't even let the kid keep the ten dollars, not at first."

Burns stripped off the itchy beard. "I don't see how you can be so sure about her. I've read that shoplifting is like a disease. You never know who might have it. And since we're doing "A Christmas Carol," I've been thinking about Dickens. She's probably a Fagin."

"What's a Fagin?"

"Who. Who's a Fagin. He's a character in *Oliver Twist*. He has a bunch of kids who do his thieving for him."

"You think *Larry* is doing the lifting?"

Burns shook his head. "Not really. To be honest, she's the only one I saw today who even looked the least bit suspicious. There's just no way anyone could be stealing stuff from this store."

"Sure there is," Napier said. "You just haven't given it enough time."

"Yes I have," Burns said. He threw the red cap on top of the pile he had made of the Santa outfit. "I've found out I don't have a flair for investigative work after all. I quit."

The first performance of "A Christmas Carol" was very well received. Many of the prominent members of the community were in attendance, including Franklin Miller, the president of Hartley Gorman College, who took the time to congratulate Burns on his reading.

"Excellent, Burns, excellent," Miller said, shaking Burns' hand. "This has been just wonderful for college and community relations."

His remarks didn't make Burns feel any better. Elaine had been ignoring him ever since the episode at Cameron's, though Burns had tried to put the best face possible on things when he explained to her why he had given up the job. He could tell that she was disappointed in him, however, and there was no telling what Napier might have said to her about why Burns was off the job.

Burns looked over the departing audience and saw several other people he knew. There was Marion Everson, editor of Pecan City's almost-daily newspaper; Gene Vale, president of the Chamber of Commerce; and several HGC faculty members, including Mal Tomlin and Earl Fox.

Even Jay Cameron was there. It was eight-thirty, and the storeowner would just have time to get to his place of business before closing time for one last check of the premises. The shoplifters still had not been caught. Cameron, however, had not been sorry to see Burns resign as Santa. It was as if he was more willing to suffer his losses than to have Burns make another scene. Burns didn't blame him for feeling that way.

Then Burns had a thought. He walked over to where Napier was graciously accepting the congratulations of an admiring Elaine Tanner and several others for his sensitive interpretation of Tiny Tim.

Burns waited until Napier looked his way and indicated that he would like a word with the Chief. Napier shook a few more hands, laughed, and made his way to Burns, looking back to smile at Elaine over his shoulder.

Burns tried not to grind his teeth. "I think I've cracked the case," he said when Napier reached him.

"What case?" Napier said.

"You know what case."

"Oh, *that* case. I thought you quit."

"I did, but I've been thinking about it."

"Thinking about it. You cracked it by thinking about it? Like Sherlock Holmes?"

Burns smiled. "More like C. Auguste Dupin."

Napier thought about that. "Who?" he said.

"Never mind," Burns said. "Just meet me at Cameron's at nine o'clock."

"Tonight?" Napier said, looking at his watch.

"Right. In fact, why don't we go in your car?"

"You're not going to make more trouble are you?"

"Who, me?" Burns said. "Of course not."

"You better not," Napier said. "If you do, I'll sic Mrs. Branton on you."

"Ha ha," Burns said. But he wasn't being jolly.

Burns and Napier sat in the squad car. Not wanting to alert anyone to their presence, Napier refused to leave the motor on and run the heater. He even rolled his window down a half-inch and made Burns do the same so the windows wouldn't fog over. Burns was freezing. He rubbed his hands together and stuck them between his thighs to warm them.

Napier hummed the theme from *Hawaii Five-O*, tapping on the steering wheel to keep time.

"I wish you wouldn't hum that song," Burns said. "It bothers me."

"Those Five-O guys are my heroes," Napier said, thinking of warm surf and swaying palm trees. "You better be right about this, Burns. You know that?"

"I'm right. How much did you say the store lost the day I was there?"

"Four thousand. Little more. You stretch that out over three or four weeks, it mounts up."

The last customers left the store. Mrs. Branton and Larry. This time Mrs. Branton was carrying a bulging shopping bag. A salesclerk locked the door behind her.

"There she is," Burns said. "She sure does have a heavy purse."

"But she's not a thief," Napier said.

"I know that now," Burns said.

They waited in the car while balances were checked against the stock, Cameron no doubt moaning over his latest losses. The clerks began to trickle out.

Finally Cameron himself came out. The store was dark now, and Cameron carefully checked the door before he started across the parking lot to his car. He was wearing a bulky topcoat over his expensive suit.

"Now?" Napier said.

"Now or never," Burns said, opening his door and getting out.

They met Cameron just as he reached his car.

"Good evening, Chief. Dr. Burns," Cameron said. "I enjoyed your performance this evening."

Napier thanked him.

"And what brings you my way?" Cameron said.

"Well," Napier said, "Burns has this crazy idea that he knows who's been stealing from your store."

"He does?" Cameron said. "That's good news."

"Not so good," Napier said. "He thinks it's you."

Cameron seemed to pale under the glow of the lamps that lighted the parking lot. "Me?" he said.

"You," Burns said. "Chief Napier said it couldn't be your employees. You were too careful for that. And I sat there all day and never saw anyone take a thing. I thought I did, but I didn't. And neither did any of your professionals. So if no one was taking anything, that left only one person, one person who visited every department and had every opportunity to take whatever he wanted. You."

"I don't see how you could think such a thing," Cameron said, tucking his coat around him.

"Why don't you show us what's under the coat?" Napier said. "If there's nothing, then Burns was just wrong. Again."

"Of course he's wrong. I never heard of anything so outrageous. Why would I steal from my own store?"

"Money," Burns said. "The store's in trouble, but if you stole from yourself, you could collect twice. Once from the insurance company and once from the fence you sold the merchandise to. It makes sense to me."

"Me too," Napier said. "Open the coat." He reached out

115

as if to pull open the front of the topcoat, and Cameron jerked away. A small bag dropped on the asphalt of the parking lot.

Burns grabbed it before Cameron could bend down. He opened it and looked inside. "Watches," he said. "Did you remember to pay for these, Mr. Cameron?"

Napier didn't appear interested in the watches. "Got anything else under that coat, Cameron?" he said.

Cameron looked at Burns, then at Napier. His face set itself for a second, then collapsed. He opened the coat to reveal several other sacks of merchandise tucked here and there.

Napier shook his head. "Looks like you were right, Burns. I hate to admit it, but maybe you do have a flair for this kind of thing, after all."

Burns smiled. "Book him, Tim-o," he said.

A werewolf detective? Hey, why not? This is actually the first of two stories about the same characters, as the ending of this one makes clear. After you read it, you'll know the true story of Little Red Riding Hood.

It Happened at Grandmother's House

1

I never asked to be a werewolf. Oh, sure, it has its compensations, but not nearly enough of them.

Take adolescence, for example. You think zits and raging hormones are a problem? Throw in the fact that you turn into a wolf every time there's a full moon, and you have a guy who's really in trouble when it comes to getting dates.

Some of you women are thinking, "Hey, no big deal. I've dated guys like that." No, you haven't. I'm not responsible for what the more or less normal teenage guy does when the moon is full, which I'm sure is bad enough. But for me it was a lot worse. Trying to convince someone that you just have a bit of excessive chest hair isn't the best way to establish a romantic relationship.

Yes, it's not easy being a teenage werewolf, and if you've ever seen that movie with Michael Landon, you know what I mean. Then there's that other movie, *Teen Wolf.* Sure, everyone loves Michael J. Fox because he's such a great basketball player, but sports never worked out that well for me. You think it's hard to dribble or throw a pass with your hands? Just try it with paws sometime.

But this isn't about a movie. It's about real life, or what passes for it in my case, and about something that happened to me when I was in high school.

It all started with a girl named Marie Grayson. I was very interested in girls at the time, in spite of the difficulties caused by my unusual proclivities, and this one had red hair. I was always a sucker for redheads, at least when I wasn't Changed. Then I was a sucker for schnauzers, but that's another story. There was one once . . . Never mind.

Back to the redhead. Marie. She also had that perfect complexion that sometimes goes along with red hair. Rhonda Fleming had it. Not to mention Maureen O'Hara. And she had long legs and green eyes and soft breasts—at least I imagined they were soft. I certainly never got close enough to judge for myself.

I did get close enough to talk to her, though, and that was good enough for me. I never really expected any more. Just an occasional smile and a pat on the head—that's all I asked.

And that's all I got, until the time, possibly inspired by having drunk one too many root beers, I talked a little bit too much and told her the truth about myself.

She laughed, of course. Wouldn't you?

"A werewolf?" she said. "You?"

We were sitting in my car, a nowhere-new 1970 Ford Fairlane, at the Root Beer Stand: "All drinks served in frosted mugs!" She was leaning against the passenger door so hard I thought she might fall out. It might have been my imagination, but I thought she was leaning even harder since my unguarded confession.

I took a sip of my third root beer from the no-longer frosty mug and nodded sadly. "That's right. A werewolf. The genuine article. It's my grandfather's fault."

"Your grandfather?"

"Right. He was the one who went to Tibet and got bitten. I guess he had no idea a bite like that could affect his genetic structure. Anyway, that's how it happened."

Her green eyes sparkled in the light from all the bulbs lining the Root Beer Stand's awning. She was drinking pink lemonade.

"So your father's a werewolf, too."

"No," I said. "My mother."

"Oh, good grief."

"I know it's hard to believe," I said. "But it's true." I took another sip of root beer. "She'd kill me if she knew I'd told."

"Kill you?"

"Well, I don't mean that literally. At least I don't *think* I do. You never can tell what might happen during the Change."

"Tell me about that," she said.

"Well, once she Changed a day early. It can happen. And of course she hadn't taken the usual precautions—"

"I don't mean about what your mother might do to you. I mean about the Change. That's what I want to hear about."

"Oh."

"You don't have to say it like that. I care about you and what might happen when your mother Changes too soon, but what I'd really like to know is what it's like."

So I told her. It's pretty unpleasant, and I won't go into it here, except to say that it hurts. A lot. Every part of you hurts, even your hair.

"So I've decided never to have children," I finished. "It wouldn't be fair. I wouldn't want them to go through all the stuff I've had to."

She looked at me and said, "You really believe it, don't you. You really believe that you're a werewolf."

"Why not? You think it's some kind of joke? It's not. I could prove it to you, but I won't. I'd never let anyone see me Change."

"I don't think I'd enjoy it, anyway."

"*I* don't enjoy it, that's for sure."

She finished off her lemonade and handed the empty mug to me. I set it on the tray that the carhop had attached to my lowered window.

Marie gave me a speculative look. "So if you're really a werewolf—"

"I am."

"—if you're really a werewolf, you're kind of like a dog, I guess."

"What's that supposed to mean?"

"You don't have to look that way. I didn't mean anything bad. I just assumed that you'd have some kind of special senses. Like being able to find your way back home if you were accidentally moved across country."

Obviously she'd been watching too many Disney movies. On the other hand, she might have a point.

"I probably could," I said.

"And I'll bet you have a great sense of smell."

"White Shoulders," I said.

"Thank you."

"I was talking about perfume."

"Oh. I'm not wearing perfume."

"I didn't mean you. I meant the girl in the car next to us. On your side."

She glanced over her shoulder. "There's an empty space next to us."

"But there's a car next to the space."

"OK. I see it, and there's someone in it, all right. But how do I find out if you're right about the perfume?"

I shrugged. "You could ask her."

So she did. When she got back in the car, she was looking at me with something that might have been respect, but it might also have been suspicion.

"This isn't some kind of set-up is it?" she said.

"Why would I want to set you up?"

"I don't know. Guys do stuff like that. And this werewolf business just seems . . . weird."

"You should see it from where I am."

She didn't say anything, just sat and leaned against the door and thought about something. I put my empty mug on the tray. The carhop came and picked up the tray and her measly tip.

"There's someone I'd like for you to meet," Marie said after a while.

"Meet? Why?"

"I think she'd find you interesting. And maybe there's something you could help her with."

"Her?"

"My grandmother," she said.

2

There are all kinds of neighborhoods in Houston. When you drive north over the Pierce Elevated and look to the right, you see the concrete canyons of downtown. Towering office buildings glitter so close to the highway that it seems you could almost touch them if you stuck your arm out the window.

Look to the left, however, just a little farther along, and it's a different story. You can see squatty old buildings with shattered windows and decaying houses that look as if they haven't been painted since the stock market took that little tumble back in 1929.

Marie's grandmother's house wasn't in either of those places. It was out near the Galleria, in another kind of area, one that had practically been out in the country when the house was built but which was now covered up by apartment houses and condos.

It was a low ranch-style that sat on a big corner lot, shaded by oak trees with branches so heavy and thick with leaves that there was almost no grass growing beneath them. The smooth, nearly bare ground was covered with tiny acorns, and a couple of squirrels chased each other around the trunk of one of the trees.

The squirrels were funny, and I smiled, which was a mistake. The smile pulled my lips back from my teeth just a little and gave Marie the wrong idea.

"You're not going to do anything . . . funny, are you?"

I looked at her, then at the squirrels. "I'm not going to jump out and chase them, if that's what you mean. The moon won't be full for another three days. I've never Changed that early before, so you don't have to worry."

"Oh. Well, I'm sorry I said anything. I didn't mean to offend you."

"I'm not offended," I told her, but my feelings were hurt all the same.

Marie reached into the back seat for the paper bag she'd brought with her, and we got out of the car. The bag was heavy, and Marie cradled it in both arms as we went up the concrete walk to the front door. The walk, which never got any sunshine, was dark with mildew, and the bronze doorknob was black with corrosion. Since Marie's hands were full, I rang the bell.

I don't know what I was expecting. Probably someone like my own grandmother, who was in her late sixties but who looked around ninety. At least to me.

Marie's grandmother wasn't like that at all. In the heavy shade of the oaks, she didn't look much older than Marie.

Her hair was almost white, but not white like my grandmother's. It was blonde, the kind of blonde you bought at the Walgreen's in a peroxide bottle. And she was hardly wrinkled at all. Her eyes were green, like Marie's, and she was wearing a shirt that showed off her breasts almost as well as her tight Levi's showed off the rest of her. She was also wearing Chanel No. 5, but then I'd suspected that ever since we'd parked at the curb.

"Hi, Grandma," Marie said. "Here's your bag of goodies." She handed her the paper bag, and then introduced her to me as Helen Grayson.

"Pleased to meet you," I said, wondering if it was all right to lust after someone's grandmother. I was pretty sure it wasn't, but I was a teenager, and there wasn't much I could do about it.

"Come on in," she said. "I'll shake your hand as soon as I put these books down."

We followed her into the sunken den, where two walls were completely covered with bookshelves. The shelves were crammed with all kinds of books, hardbacks and paperbacks. Most of them were mysteries.

"Marie's mother and I love to read," Mrs. Grayson said.

She set the bag on a low coffee table that sat in front of a floral couch. Then she turned to me and stuck out her hand. I took it and felt almost as if a spark jumped between us. I tried not to show anything, but I probably did. I must have because out of the corner of my eye I saw Marie smirking.

"I'm really glad you could come," Mrs. Grayson said, dropping my hand. "Why don't we all have a seat, and then we can talk."

She and Marie sat on the couch, so rather than fling myself between them, which I would dearly have loved to do, I sat in an old Kennedy rocker. It was a lot like one my own grandmother had, and just as uncomfortable.

"So," Mrs. Grayson said after we were all settled, "Marie tells me that you have some . . . unusual abilities."

I looked at Marie.

"I didn't tell her anything specific," she said. "I just said that you might be able to help her out with a problem she's having."

"I'd be glad to try," I said, wondering what I could possibly do for a woman like that. Maybe her back yard needed mowing or something. I didn't much like mowing, but I'd do it if that's what she wanted. I probably would have done just about anything.

"I'd like for you to smell something," she said.

I goggled at her, and she laughed. She had a nice laugh, so nice that I almost wasn't embarrassed. Almost.

"My, what big eyes you have," she said.

I felt my face starting to burn, and I opened my mouth to say something. I'm not sure what, since nothing came out, which was no doubt just as well.

"It's just a piece of paper," Marie said. She sounded a little put out with me. "Show him, Grandmother."

Mrs. Grayson got up, smiled at me, and glided out of the room. She was back before my face had even had time to return to its normal color, and she handed me a folded piece of lined notebook paper just like the kind everyone uses in school.

I took it and unfolded it. There was printing on it, big block letters all done in pencil:

I'VE BEEN WATCHING YOU, I LIKE YOU A LOT, I THINK YOU'D LIKE ME TOO IF YOU'D GIVE IT A CHANCE.

"Uh-oh," I said.

"Indeed," Mrs. Grayson said. "It's scary, isn't it."

"The punctuation is bad, too," I said.

"I don't think that's the problem," Marie said. "There's another one."

Mrs. Grayson handed me another folded paper. I read that one, too.

I THINK YOU'RE HOT, I'VE GOT SOMETHING FOR YOU, YOU'RE GOING TO LIKE IT A LOT.

That was so bad that I didn't even feel like commenting on the attempt at poetry, which after all could have been an accident.

"Who wrote these?" I said.

"There are more," Mrs. Grayson said.

"And they're worse," Marie added.

I didn't think I wanted to see them. I said that they hadn't answered my question.

"We don't know," Mrs. Grayson said. "That's what I want you to tell me."

"I don't think you want me. I think you want the police."

"I've had the police. They took the other notes, but they haven't been able to do a thing. You can buy notebook paper like this all over the city, and apparently there are no fingerprints."

"How did you get the notes?"

Mrs. Grayson smiled at me, and I started getting warm again.

"That's a very good question. Someone slipped them under my back door."

"Then get the cops to watch the house. That's the best way to catch him."

"They watched. They even stayed in the house, but they

didn't catch him. When they were here, he didn't show up. When they left, he slipped the notes under the back door again."

The back yard had a six-foot high wooden fence around it. Whoever was writing the notes must have been pretty athletic.

"The police believe that whoever is writing these notes is someone I know," Mrs. Grayson said, "maybe someone from the neighborhood."

"That's where you come in," Marie said. "I thought maybe you could smell the note and tell us who wrote it."

"Oh, good grief," I said.

After they explained things, however, I realized the idea wasn't quite as dumb as it sounded. If I could pick up a scent from the paper, which I admitted was a possibility, though not a very good one since a lot of people besides the writer had handled it and since the writer had probably been wearing gloves, I might be able to match the scent to one of the neighbors. Assuming one of the neighbors was the writer. It all seemed pretty thin to me.

"It's about all we've got, though," Mrs. Grayson said. "The police are no help at all. I think whoever wrote these notes would have to kill me for them to get really interested in doing anything. To tell the truth, I'm getting frightened."

I didn't blame her. "What if it's not someone from the neighborhood?" I said. "What if it's some nut from out of town?"

"I don't think that's very likely, do you?"

"No," I admitted. And then I had another thought. "What if I do find out who wrote the notes? What are you going to do then?"

"Why, I'm going to tell the police, of course."

"That would never work," I said "Not in a million years."

"Why not?" she asked, so I told her.

Well, I didn't actually tell her. What I said was that the cops weren't going to believe some kid who said he'd smelled a man's scent on a piece of paper. I didn't add that they wouldn't believe me even if I told them that I was a werewolf. If they believed that part, they'd probably run out looking for silver bullets.

Mrs. Grayson looked disappointed, but she knew I was right.

"I'm sorry I couldn't help," I said, and I meant it.

"Maybe you still could," Marie said, looking thoughtful. She looked good that way, but then she looked good most ways. Genetics was bad news when it came to werewolves, but she and her grandmother were certainly proof that nothing is all bad.

"How?" I asked.

"Instead of the police watching the house, *you* could watch it."

"Me?" I said, and then I caught on. "Oh. Yeah. Me."

"Am I missing something?" Mrs. Grayson asked.

"Not really," I said.

While I was taking her home, Marie filled me in on her plan.

"You'd do it during the time of the full moon, of course. I'll bet wolves know all kinds of ways to hide out in the dark."

"It's not so dark when the moon is full," I pointed out.

"You know what I mean. You're probably very sly when you're a wolf."

I wasn't ever very sly, but of course I couldn't tell her that. I was still hoping to impress her.

"And you could still check out the men in the neighborhood," she said. "That way, you'd know who to expect, and you'd know where he was coming from."

"Let's say, just for the sake of argument, that I do this. What am I supposed to do if the guy actually shows up? Rip his throat out?"

Marie shuddered. "Would you really do that?"

"I'm not sure," I admitted. "I don't think so, though. I've sure never done anything like that before."

Well, except for a chicken one time, but I didn't think it would be tactful to mention that. It was more in the way of an experiment than anything else, and it hadn't been exactly pleasant.

So I just said, "I don't think I'd like the taste of blood."

"Yuck. I wish you wouldn't talk like that."

"You started it."

"Maybe. But what I meant was that maybe you could . . . bark at him. Do wolves bark?"

"No. And that wouldn't scare anybody, anyway."

"How about if you jumped up on him? Knocked him down, maybe, and then slobbered in his face. Growled. Showed him your fangs. You have fangs, don't you?"

I had fangs, all right, and pretty big ones, but I didn't think that would work, either.

Marie said, "He'd think she had some kind of giant watch dog. He'd probably never come back. And if he did, we could file a complaint with the police. You could identify him and say you saw him put the note under the door. It would be the truth, too, sort of."

OK, it was possible. Barely. But so are a lot of things. I said I'd think about it. I didn't want to disappoint Marie. Or her grandmother, for that matter.

"I want to know now," Marie said.

"Why?"

"So I'll know whether to give you a kiss when we get to my house."

I didn't need to think any longer. "I'll do it," I said.

She smiled. "I thought you might."

3

I spent a lot of time in my room that night, sniffing notebook paper. It didn't do any good, though. Mostly, I could smell Mrs. Grayson's perfume, and there was a faint odor of something that was probably leather. You'd think that whoever wrote the notes would use some kind of gloves that would be more flexible—rubber, for example. And there was another odor, even more faint, of something that smelled like new houses. Unless the writer was a carpenter, I didn't have a thing to go on.

That didn't discourage Marie. She talked to me every day at school, and she called me in the evenings. I had to admit that I didn't mind the attention. Maybe I should have mentioned to her sooner that I was a werewolf.

On the day of the night of the full moon, she caught up with me in the hall near my locker. The hall was noisy, as usual, with locker doors clanging, guys talking loud, feet shuffling, and Marie put her mouth close to my ear so I could hear her.

"Are you going to watch the house tonight?"

Her warm breath tickled my ear, and I was afraid I might turn into a wolf right then and there, even though I'd never Changed in the daylight hours before. And I didn't that time, either, but it was a near thing.

"I guess so," I said.

"Can I come too?"

She was fascinated with the idea of the Change, but I

wasn't about to let her see it. She might think it would be exciting, but it's not. It's mostly just ugly and painful.

"No," I said. "It's too dangerous."

"Pleeease."

"Forget it. If you try to come, I won't do it."

She pouted, sticking out a lovely, full lower lip, but it didn't do her any good.

"Oh, all right," she said after a minute. "What's your plan?"

"I don't have one," I said.

And I didn't. In the first place, I didn't think anyone would show up. There hadn't been any new notes since I'd visited Mrs. Grayson, and there was no real reason to think one would arrive that evening. They had come at irregular intervals from the beginning. But I'd said I'd watch, so I would.

After school that day I went home and told my mother I was going out that night.

"I don't think so," she said. "You know the rules."

The rules were pretty standard. She and I both had agreed to them long ago. During the full moon, we stayed home, in our rooms, which had been fixed up to be more or less werewolf proof.

We didn't really need the precautions—bars on the windows, thick wall hangings, doors that my father locked from the outside—because we weren't at all like the werewolves in most of the movies you've seen. We were basically domesticated and didn't have any desire to mangle human flesh, though there were enough animal instincts to make us dangerous to chickens now and then and (as I found out later) interested in Schnauzers and the like. Mostly we spent the nights of the Change sleeping or watching TV. Even a wolf can do that.

I explained to my mother that I was just going to do a favor for a friend. She didn't think it was a good idea.

"Werewolves don't do favors," she said. "We just keep out of sight and mind our own business."

I told her that there was a girl involved, and that really set her off.

"You haven't *told* her, have you? You know what could happen if you did that. Or maybe you don't, but you certainly should. It will be the peasants and the torches all over again."

"I thought that was Frankenstein."

"Don't you get smart with your mother."

I apologized and tried to explain what I was going to do.

"You're just going to watch the house?"

I said that was the plan.

"And you're sure that's all?"

I said I was sure, though I really had no idea.

"Well, I don't like the idea of a woman being tormented like that. She doesn't have protection like you and I do. Why if a man tried that on me, I'd rip him to shreds."

I said that I didn't doubt it. "Does that mean I can go?"

"I suppose so. But you be careful. You never know who might be using silver bullets these days."

"I'll be careful."

"And get back before dawn. You know what happens if you're out at dawn."

I knew. Cinderella had nothing on us werewolves.

"And don't tell your father. I'll handle him."

That was fine with me. I wasn't sure my father had ever completely adjusted to having a werewolf wife, much less a teenage werewolf son.

"Will you need any help?"

"I don't think so," I said.

Little did I know.

4

The moon came up big and bright, or as big and bright as it gets in the city, and I knew about it before anyone else. Except for my mother, of course, and any other werewolves that might be around. We don't know of any. And we don't have to see the moon. The Change happens when it's raining or when there's an eclipse or when you're in a sealed basement. It doesn't have anything to do with light.

As I said, it's painful. My bones stretch, my skull changes shape, my mouth fills with sharp white fangs, my nails become claws while my feet and hands are becoming padded paws.

Sometimes I howl.

Not this time, however. It wouldn't have been a good idea. I wasn't in my room like most of the times before. I was on a tree-covered lot, not far from Mrs. Grayson's house. I could tell by some stakes with red ribbons on them that the lot had recently been surveyed, and it wouldn't be long before someone built a house there, but right now it was perfect for my purposes.

Lots of people think of Texas in general as a part of the southwestern desert, and parts of it are. But Houston is a coastal city with a sub-tropical climate. One of the things that sometimes surprises people who visit for the first time is the number of trees. They're all over the place, and the ones on the lot provided me with plenty of cover for Changing.

It doesn't take long, which is a good thing considering how painful it is, and before the moon had really gotten into the sky I was a wolf. Not a bad looking one, either, if I do say so myself. Big, black, and hairy, true, but not unattractive if you happened to be another wolf. Or even a Schnauzer.

The smells of the city came to me much more sharply after I Changed—diesel oil, exhaust fumes, the hot pavement, and even the cool smell of the oak trees that I was sheltering among. I could feel the grass cool under my paws and hear a bird rustling in the branches over my head.

I waited until it was as dark as it was going to get and trotted off to Mrs. Grayson's. I wasn't really worried about being seen. I figured that anyone who happened to catch sight of me would think I was just a big black dog on his way home, and there were plenty of shadows to duck into if I had to escape the animal control officer.

I circled Mrs. Grayson's block, sniffing around all the houses. A couple of times dogs penned in back yards barked in alarm, but the owners didn't notice.

There were no new houses on the block. All of them were as old as Mrs. Grayson's, and I was a bit disappointed. I'd hoped that finding the owner of the gloves might turn out to be easy. Oh, well.

Keeping myself in the shadows, I got a running start and jumped Mrs. Grayson's fence. It was easy for a wolf, though I thought a man might have a problem.

I sniffed around the back yard but didn't find anything unusual. A possum had been there recently, and some squirrels were living in one of the trees, but that was all. No scent of man.

I could smell perfume, of course, but that was coming from inside the house. A back window glowed with light, and I wondered if it was Mrs. Grayson's bedroom. I wondered if she knew I was out there. Or cared.

I circled the yard three or four times and lay down by a woodpile to wait. I stretched out my paws in front of me and rested my chin on them. I was sure it was going to be a long night, and there was nothing to entertain me except the squirrels, who were asleep, and the bugs in the woodpile, who didn't interest me.

After only a few minutes, I got restless. I got up and sniffed around the woodpile, thinking that maybe bugs wouldn't be such bad companions after all. I could hear them skittering around in there, and I sniffed at the logs.

I smelled something familiar almost at once, and I realized that I probably knew who had put those notes under Mrs. Grayson's door. If I was right, he was even more dangerous than we'd thought. Several Houston women had been raped and murdered over the last few months, in ways that were remarkably similar, and the police were baffled. All the murders had occurred at the time of the full moon, which wasn't unusual for that kind of killer. The women had no connection with one another as far as anyone had been able to figure out. Up until now, anyway. I thought I'd figured it out, and all I had to do was tell Mrs. Grayson.

But there was a slight problem with that idea. Wolves can't tell anybody anything. We might look a little like Lassie, but the resemblance is purely physical. We don't have her ability to communicate. Little Timmy would just have to drown in the well if things were left to us.

I was so excited that I didn't think about that, however. I wanted to let Mrs. Grayson know that I'd solved her problem, and maybe I even had some idea that she'd be so grateful to me that she'd scratch me behind the ears. It's possible that I was even thinking that she might be wearing some kind of filmy nightgown and that I might have a chance to nuzzle her here and there while she scratched my head.

I'm sure that if I hadn't been muddled by thoughts of pleasurable rewards for my efforts, I would have heard someone coming over the fence, though he must have been awfully quiet.

And I'm sure I would have heard him sneaking up behind me if I hadn't already been scratching frantically at the back door. I might even have heard him pick up a log from the woodpile.

Or maybe I would have smelled him if I hadn't been a little too conscious of the odor of Chanel No. 5 that oozed out from under Mrs. Grayson's back door.

I smelled him before I heard him, though, and I tried to turn. I heard him, too, but it was too late.

What I heard was his voice saying, "Good night, poochie."

And then he slammed me in the head with the log.

5

I don't know how long I lay sprawled out by the back door, but I'm sure it wasn't long, no more than a few seconds. We were-wolves have pretty thick skulls, thicker than most dogs and humans, and that's probably what saved me.

I was groggy, and my head was beating like a tympani, but I was alive. That was all that mattered, that and the fact that the door was slightly ajar. In his rush to get inside, the man who'd hit me hadn't closed it all the way. I could hear noises from the house, as if someone were smashing furniture.

I was afraid that my legs might be too shaky to hold me up, but they worked more or less all right. I nosed the door farther open and staggered inside.

The noise was coming from the room where the light had been in the window, so I headed that way, wagging my head from side to side in an attempt to clear it. Drops of blood spattered on the tile floor of the kitchen. I was sure that wasn't a good sign, but I kept going.

Soon enough I was at the door of a back bedroom. A tall

man wearing jeans, scuffed boots, and a denim jacket was throwing himself against the closet door. He had on leather work gloves, too.

"You might's well come on out of there, sweet mama," he said.

There was no sound from inside the closet, and he braced himself before slamming his shoulder into the door. He had black, oily hair, and his teeth pulled back from his lips in a fierce grimace at the crack of the wood. He looked almost as much like a wolf as I did.

"One more time, honey," he said. "And then you're all mine. It might go easier for you if you just came on out."

There was no answer from inside the closet, but I made a low noise in my throat. The man looked around. He seemed surprised to see me.

"Well if it ain't the poochie. I didn't think I'd be hearing from you again."

He started across the room toward me. I snarled, but not very impressively. I don't suppose I was looking very wolfish. He wasn't scared at all.

"I guess I'll have to finish what I started," he said, reaching behind his back.

When I could see his hand again, it was holding a little revolver, and it was aimed right between my eyes.

Big woop. He didn't know who he was dealing with. Or what. He might be able to bash me to death with a log, though I doubted even that, and he certainly wasn't going to be able to kill me with lead bullets. My head was already feeling better, and I thought it was beginning to heal itself.

He had no way of knowing all that, however, so he pulled the trigger.

The bullet knocked me backward, and I blacked out again. I was probably out a little longer this time, because I completely missed Marie's entrance into the house. She must have come in through the garage, because she had a hatchet in her hand, and she was standing between me and the guy with the gun.

"Put the gun down," she said. "Or you'll be sorry."

The guy laughed. I didn't blame him. I almost laughed myself. But you had to hand it to Marie. She had guts.

"You're the one who's gonna be sorry," he said. "Or maybe not. Maybe you'll enjoy it. In fact, I might just leave old blondie in the closet while you and I have at it."

I couldn't let him talk to Marie like that. I stood up.

This time he was *really* surprised.

"I'll be Goddamned," he said.

He was probably right about that.

I was even shakier than I had been, but this time I didn't let that bother me. I gathered what strength I had and jumped for his throat.

He shot me twice before I hit him, but not in any area as susceptible as my head. We hit the floor in a pile, and two more bullets jolted into me. That made five. I wondered if he carried one under the hammer.

He didn't. I heard a couple of clicks, and then he began hitting me in the head with the butt of the gun while I tried to bite him with absolutely no success. He was jerking around too much.

The shots hardly affected me, but the blows from the pistol butt did. After all, I'd been shot in the head and hit with a log. It was a little tender.

I whined and rolled off him. He jumped up and started kicking me in the head. I howled. Maybe he *could* kill me by beating me to a pulp.

He didn't, though, because Marie split him open with the hatchet.

137

She told the police later that it was an accident, and I believe that it was. She threw the hatchet at him, hoping he'd be distracted and stop hurting me. How was she to know that it would turn over just right and that the blade would meet his forehead just above the nose?

When she saw what she'd done, she got sick all over the rug, and she was sitting on the edge of the bed, still heaving, when Mrs. Grayson came out of the closet.

6

The newspapers got it all wrong, of course, or most of them did. The way they told it, Mrs. Grayson had been attacked by a vicious wolf, and a heroic handyman had tried to save her. His own death was a tragic accident, and the severely wounded wolf had escaped. Readers should beware of vicious sneak attacks.

Geez.

I didn't escape, exactly. I must have looked dead when the cops got there, which was a lot sooner than you'd think. A neighbor had heard the shots and called them. I was still lying on the floor when they arrived, and they ignored me.

Marie told me later that she got me out of there and into the yard in all the confusion. Of course the fact that Mrs. Grayson was dressed in the scanty nightie that I'd imagined for her helped a lot. The cops couldn't keep their eyes off her. I think they forgot about me for quite a while.

And then there was the dead man, another little distraction for them to worry about.

Marie told them that I'd jumped up and run out of the room on my own, and they didn't doubt her. For weeks there were wolf sightings all over the city.

Nobody actually saw me, of course. I recovered in the yard

and got out of there as soon as I figured out that I was no longer needed. I'd done my part about as well as I could.

I explained my theory to Marie later, and she confirmed that I was right. The guy was a handyman, and he also sold firewood by the cord. He cut it somewhere in the country and brought it into town in an old truck, which the police had found parked several blocks from the house.

The "new-house" smell I'd noticed on the paper had been sawdust, of course, and my idea was that the guy would case houses where he sold the wood. If there was a woman living alone, and she had a fireplace that she liked to use a couple of times in the winter, she was in danger if she bought wood from the wrong guy.

Marie told the police the theory, saying it was her own, and they checked it out. Four of the five women who had been killed had bought wood from the guy, according to their neighbors, and the fifth might have. There was wood in her yard, but no one knew where it had come from. So the cops could close the books on the killer.

I was upset with Marie for having been at the house, even if she had pretty much saved my life.

"I can't believe you're so ungrateful," she said.

"It's not that. But you put yourself in danger."

"I just wanted to see you change. But you cheated. You weren't there."

"I had a feeling you might be hiding around. And I didn't want to Change there, anyway. Where did you get that hatchet, by the way?"

"I waited for you in the back yard for a long time before I decided that you weren't coming. Then I went to my car and listened to the radio for a while, thinking that if you wouldn't watch the house, I would. When I heard the shots, I came inside. I didn't know where the front door key was, but I knew that my grandmother kept a key to the garage door in her washing machine in the garage. There was a hatchet on the old workbench that my grandfather used before he died, so I just grabbed it."

"I'm glad you did."

"I'm not so sure that I am."

She'd get over it, but I didn't say that. What I said was, "The moon's not full tonight. We could go to a movie or something."

"I don't think so," she said. "I'm still too upset about everything that's happened."

I could understand that. I'd been a little upset, too, and my mother had grounded me for a week when she saw my head. It looked fine now, however.

I was sorry that Marie didn't want to go to a movie with me. Maybe she would later on and we could live happily ever after. Or maybe her curiosity about werewolves was wearing off. I was afraid that might be the case.

I wondered if her grandmother would like to see a movie, but I didn't think I should ask. We hadn't told her grandmother about my brave confrontation with the killer, and since she'd been in the closet she had no idea that I'd even been there. Even if she'd seen me she wouldn't have known it was me. So I didn't have much leverage with her.

Oh, well. That's the way it is when you're a werewolf. You hardly ever get credit for anything. Marie and I sort of drifted apart after that, and after graduation I didn't see her again for years. We did meet again, however, but that's another story, to be told another time.

In case you were wondering what happens when the werewolf detective grows older (and even if you weren't), here's the answer.

The Nighttime Is the Right Time

It's not easy being a werewolf.

In the first place, no matter what the song says, your hair's not perfect. At least mine's not. It looks a lot like David Letterman's hair, and that's *before* the Change. When the Change happens, I look more like a white German Shepherd whose mother was scared by a Malamute with an incipient case of the mange.

I won't even mention the fleas except to say that anything you pick up while you're Changed, you keep when you resume your human form.

Look in your medicine cabinet. What do you see?

Never mind. That doesn't matter. Let me tell you what you *don't* see: You don't see a bottle of Dr. Glover's Mange Cure or a pump spray bottle of Hartz Mountain Flea Spray For Dogs, both of which are in my own medicine cabinet, although hidden pretty much out of sight.

But I don't want you to think I spend all my time feeling sorry for myself.

On the contrary, I have a pretty good life, ever since the time I saved Red Riding Hood's grandmother from that crazy axe murderer who'd been eking out a living as a woodchopper while on the dodge from the law in seven states.

You've probably heard the story, so I won't go into it here except to say that as usual the news media screwed it all up. Naturally they had to make the wolf the villain. We hardly ever get any good notices from the media.

Not that I really blame the press and the TV news reporters. It would have been pretty hard for anyone to believe the truth in this particular case. The *Weekly World News* might have printed it, but who would have believed it?

Red, however, knew the straight of it. I kept in touch with her over the years, and she looked me up much later to let me know that her grandmother had died a peaceful, natural death, leaving Red a tidy sum, not to mention setting aside a bit for me, too. After all, if it hadn't been for me, old Granny would have gone to her final reward about fifteen years sooner than she did. And I'm sure she realized that dying in her bed was a lot more pleasant than what that maniacal woodchopper had in mind for her.

So there we were, Red and me, at the lawyer's office for the reading of granny's will and renewing old acquaintances, which led us to stop in at a nice dark bar afterward for a wee drop of comfort.

Werewolves can handle alcohol all right, or at least I can, just as long as I don't drink it during the full moon. If I overdo it then, it's Katy bar the door. I remember this cute little female schnauzer one time . . . but that's another story.

Anyway, Red and I had a drink, and we talked about what we'd been doing since I saved old granny. Red had spent most of the time growing up and going to law school.

"Just what the world needs," I said, tipping up my glass to get the last of the gin and tonic. "Another lawyer."

"I'm not a lawyer," she said. "I'm a private eye."

Well, I was surprised. She didn't look like a private eye, at least not like the ones on TV. A Victoria's Secret model, maybe, but not a private eye. But then she didn't look like a lawyer, either.

For that matter, I probably don't look like a werewolf.

"You're kidding," I said.

"No, I'm not. I decided I didn't want to do litigation, and I didn't want to be cooped up in an office all day doing legal research or writing contracts. So I went into business for myself."

Our waitress came over and asked if we wanted another round. I looked at Red. She nodded, so I ordered another couple of gin and tonics. Got to be careful of malaria when you live in a subtropical climate like Houston's. Or that was the way my reasoning went.

"What do private eyes do?" I asked when the waitress was gone. "I guess it's not like in the movies."

She shrugged. "Sometimes it is. But mostly it's pretty dull. I do a lot of skip-tracing, and you can do that by phone and computer."

"So most of the time you're cooped up in an office."

"That's right. But there's a job I'm working on now that's different."

She gave me a speculative look. She had green eyes to go with her red hair, and I found myself looking away from her.

"As a matter of fact," she said, "I was thinking that you might be able to help me."

"Me?" I said.

The only reason I didn't laugh out loud was that the waitress brought our drinks. She set them on the table with a couple of dinky napkins and went away.

If there was ever a more unlikely prospect to help out a private eye than me, I didn't know who it could be. I like to keep to myself, out of the public eye. Sort of a lone wolf, so to speak.

Oh, sure, I do a lot of roaming around when I'm Changed, but when I'm in human form, I don't like to develop close relationships. It's sort of hard to explain to anyone about what happens to me when it's my time of the month. So I just stay away from people as much as I can. It's never bothered me.

"What made you think of me?" I asked after taking a sip of my drink. After all, Red knew my proclivities. As far as I knew, she was the only human who did.

"I think you might have some special talents that would come in handy," she said.

"I've only got one special talent," I told her. It wasn't something I liked talking about.

Red took a handful of the little goldfish crackers from a bowl in the middle of the table. "That's the talent I mean," she said, and then popped the crackers into her mouth.

I shook my head. "I don't think I want to hear about it." But to tell the truth I was curious.

"All right," she said. She took a drink. "I suppose it's time for me to go."

"I'll walk you to your car," I offered.

The sun was down by now, and downtown Houston can be a pretty strange place after dark. I should know.

Her car was a new Toyota Camry, and I observed that she must be doing all right for herself in the private snoop business.

"I am. But I could use a little help on a certain case. It's too bad that I don't have a friend who'll listen to what I have to say about it."

My curiosity got the better of me. "All right, I give in. Do you want to have dinner and tell me all about it?"

She smiled. She had a much nicer smile than I do. Mine's a little toothy.

"Let's go to Cafe Adobe," she said. "My car or yours?"

I asked her where it was, and she gave me directions. "I'll meet you there," I said.

Cafe Adobe turned out to be on Westheimer and Shepherd, not far from a gigantic bookstore that used to be a movie theater. The marquee is still outside, but now it advertises book signings instead of features filmed in Cinema-Scope.

Red had beat me to the restaurant. I found a spot in the parking lot not far from her Camry and walked across the street. She was waiting for me outside the door. She was very pretty, I thought, and that was probably the real reason I'd agreed to hear her story. I don't usually eat at trendy cafes, or any cafes. I prefer to stay at home and eat alone.

I guess I should tell you that Red's name is really Marie Grayson. And I didn't actually save her old granny from a psychopathic woodchopper, but that's close enough to the truth to do. It happened during a full moon, and I just happened to be in the neighborhood, cruising for schnauzers. Red told the newspapers that it was a big dog that saved her and her grandmother, but she knew the truth. I'd had to Change to help her call 911. She was too upset to do it herself. She was very young, after all, and there was a dead and very bloody maniac lying on the floor.

The way the papers told the story, the "big dog" didn't really save anyone. He'd been a killer German Shepherd out to slaughter everyone in his path and savage the bodies. According to the news reports, Red and her grandmother had just gotten lucky. Like I said, the media never get it right.

"Do you want to sit inside or on the patio?" Red asked me. I'll always think of her as Red, no matter what her name is.

"Inside. Got to watch out for mosquitoes." I didn't like mosquitoes any more than I liked fleas.

We went in and got seated in the No Smoking section, not that it mattered to me. My sense of smell is so good that my nose gets irritated no matter where I sit if someone lights up.

Chuck was our server. I know, not because I cared but because he told me his name. As I think I mentioned, I don't particularly like relationships with humans, much less humans I'm never going to see again.

I ordered the spinach enchiladas. Red got a chile relleno. We sat there and ate chips and red sauce until we were served. Then, while we ate, Red told me her problem.

As it turned out, maybe she was right. Maybe I *could* help her. Just this once.

"It's a missing persons case," she said. "I don't get many of those."

I could see why. The police were better equipped for that kind of thing.

"Not really," she said when I expressed my opinion. "I have access to a lot of information through my computer, and I have more time to devote to it than they do. But this is someone they've already written off."

Probably with good reason, I thought, taking a bite of spinach enchilada. I wished for a second I'd gotten one with some meat in it, but I prefer my meat uncooked. I didn't think they served enchiladas like that.

"Why have the cops written it off?" I asked.

"They tried," she said, excusing them. "They tried hard, too, because Nathan Chronister has, or had, a lot of money. But they have so many cases it's hard for them to keep up with all of them. After they haven't found someone for a few weeks, they have to move on to something else. And this is an adult we're talking about. Adults can disappear if they want to; it's not against the law. If it were a kid, it would be different."

I could see how that might be, though it seemed a little odd that the cops would stop looking for a man with a lot of money. They work pretty hard for that kind of person.

"So how did you wind up with this one after the police wrote it off?"

"Because someone saw the missing man."

"Oh. Who saw him?"

"His wife."

I sighed. "OK. Tell me all about it. But start from the beginning this time."

She did, but we had to go elsewhere for me to get the story. Just as she was about to launch into it, Chuck and his fellow servers descended on the table of some hapless man who was having a birthday. The members of his party had informed Chuck on the sly, so the poor man was being treated to a very loud, off-key rendition of "Happy Birthday." I could see Red's lips moving, but I couldn't hear her talking, so we got out of there.

The story that Red told me was this.

Nathan Chronister had been a very successful man at a time when real estate was the business to be in if you wanted to get rich quick in Houston. It wasn't that way now, but Chronister had seen the boom years drawing to an end and gotten out of the game while he was ahead. Way ahead, to the tune of millions. No one was sure how many.

I remembered reading a few things about Chronister in the newspapers. He was a good man to know, a man with money who didn't mind spreading it around for what he considered the right reasons. For him the right reasons were pretty strange. He supported some ESP research and the paranormal.

And then one day he disappeared. He didn't take a thing with him, except for what he had on him. Not a spare shirt or tie, not an extra shoe or a safety razor. Not even a checkbook or a few dollars in cash from an automated teller machine.

He was just gone.

"And the cops couldn't find him?" I asked.

We were in Red's apartment, which was really the first floor of an old house just off Greenbriar, not far from the restaurant where we'd eaten. There was some Kevin Costner movie on the TV, but we weren't watching it. I don't much like Costner, not since he killed off the title character in his screenplay for *Dances with Wolves*.

"No one could find him," Red told me. "The police had no luck at all, and his wife's hired other private eyes before me. If you're going to find a missing person, you need a little help, a paper trail, an informant, something. But there was nothing. Chronister hasn't used a credit card or cashed a check, and he hasn't gotten in touch with anyone, at least not anyone who's admitted it."

"But his wife saw him."

"That's right. She called me yesterday."

"Why did he disappear?"

I figured there had to be a reason, and maybe there was, but Red didn't know.

"His wife was a little vague about that," she said.

"Vague?"

"She said he had his reasons. I got the impression that he was afraid of something."

"Like what?"

"That's what she didn't tell me."

That seemed fishy to me. A man just ups and leaves for no reason at all? I wasn't sure I believed it, but I wasn't a trained private investigator and Red was.

So I said, "All right. Where did she see him?"

"Not far from downtown. She was going to get on the Gulf Freeway late yesterday and drove under the Pierce Elevated."

The Elevated, in case you're lucky enough never to have driven on it, is an unbelievably congested section of Interstate 45 that passes right by downtown, about on a level with the eighth or ninth story of the buildings that seem almost close enough to touch from your car window.

But Mrs. Chronister had passed under the Elevated, which meant that her husband probably hadn't been in a car. It meant something else entirely.

"Is he living under the Elevated?" I asked.

Red nodded. Her red hair caught the light and turned almost gold. For a second I almost wished she were a schnauzer.

"Not a bad place to hide, if you're a rich man," I said. "No one would look there, and you wouldn't have to answer a lot of questions."

Lots of the city's homeless congregated under the Elevated. It wouldn't be comfortable, but you'd be anonymous. You'd also be pretty unkempt.

"She's sure it was him?"

"She's sure. And she wants me to check it out."

"But you don't want to go roaming around under the Elevated at night."

"True."

I didn't blame her, and it wasn't likely that Chronister would stay there in the daylight. No one did. Everyone was out scrabbling for aluminum cans, in spite of the fact that the market was depressed right now because of an influx of aluminum from Russia; or diving in dumpsters; or working whatever street hustle they ran to stay alive.

In the evenings they started to congregate under the Elevated in their cardboard boxes, wrapping in their blankets if the night was cool, which wasn't likely at this time of year, listening to their radios if they had any batteries, and staying out of each other's way.

Red wouldn't really be in danger, though. I hadn't heard

of any muggings there. Of course I hadn't heard of any young women who'd gone roaming around there after dark, either.

"I might not be able to recognize him," Red said. "His wife says he's changed. A lot."

"But you think *I* can recognize him."

"Well . . ." She paused. "I don't want to offend you."

"Don't worry. I'm pretty thick skinned."

"Well . . ."

"Go ahead. I can take it."

"OK. You're a wolf, right?"

I couldn't deny it, but it did make me a little defensive. "Only at certain times," I said.

"We've never talked about this, but—"

"I've never talked about it with *any*body."

"I'm sorry. If you'd rather we didn't go on—"

"Never mind. Obviously it has something to do with finding Chronister. Go ahead and say it."

"Well, I was wondering if you had any . . . doggy abilities."

"Doggy abilities? What's that supposed to mean?"

"You know. Like being able to track someone by smelling of his old clothing."

"Oh. That."

"Yes. I didn't mean to embarrass you."

I wasn't really embarrassed. As a matter of fact, I could do exactly what she was talking about. Among other things. It's just that, like everything else related to my secret life, it wasn't anything I'd ever talked about.

"So you want me to locate him?"

"If you can. If you would."

For the last few years I'd been making a living as a free-lance writer. Nature articles. Editors said that I had an uncanny insight into certain aspects of animal life. Little did they know.

Anyway, it was a perfect way for me to live. I could deal with everyone by mail or modem. I could do my research the same way, except for some of the things that gave me my uncanny insights, and those didn't call for involvement with other human beings. In fact, I'd been around more people in the last few hours than I had in the last few years.

I still went out to restaurants and stores, but I didn't have to deal with people there except on a commercial basis. I could handle that. It was involvement that I didn't want. But maybe it was time I gave it a try. Looking at Red certainly made the idea seem attractive.

"I can do it," I said. "It might be fun."

I was right about the first part, but not about the second.

Chronister's wife lived in River Oaks, in a gigantic house that sat on a plot of land not much bigger than Rhode Island and probably not much more expensive to maintain. The trees were ancient, but the flowers appeared to have sprung up fresh that very afternoon, and the front lawn looked as if an army of manicurists had been at it with trimming scissors. I knew Chronister had been rich, but I didn't know he'd been *this* rich. I didn't know anybody was.

We walked several miles of sidewalk to the front door and rang the bell. I was surprised that we weren't met by a butler in full livery, but instead the door was answered by a woman in her middle thirties, wearing a pants suit that had probably set her back about half a grand at Neiman's. She had long blond hair and very blue eyes. I couldn't see why anyone married to her would want to disappear, but then I didn't know her very well.

Red introduced me to Mrs. Jane Chronister, who took us to a living room that the Houston Symphony could have rehearsed in if it hadn't been furnished like a photo from *Better*

Homes and Gardens, and we sat on chairs that cost more than I made in a year of writing nature articles. Red didn't seem a bit intimidated by the opulence, so I tried to appear nonchalant. In those surroundings, it wasn't easy.

I was so busy getting adjusted that I missed the opening of the conversation, but I snapped to it when I heard my name mentioned.

"I'm so glad you think you can help," Mrs. Chronister said to me.

"I'll have to see something your husband owned," I told her. "Preferably something he wore that hasn't been washed."

She looked puzzled, so I told her I was a kind of psychic. "I can sense the person's vibrations in his clothing," I explained.

She glanced over at Red as if to ask whether I was some kind of nut, and I thought for a minute about telling her the truth: "I'm a werewolf, lady, and I want to get your husband's scent." Somehow I managed to restrain myself.

Red shrugged apologetically. "It's the way he does things. I know it's strange, but it seems to work."

"If you say so." Mrs. Chronister rose gracefully from the couch. "I'll be right back."

When she was gone, Red turned to me. *"Vibrations?"*

"Hey, it was the only thing I could think of."

Mrs. Chronister wasn't gone long. She came back with a denim shirt that was nearly unwrinkled.

"He put this on to wear to a movie a day or two before he disappeared," she said, handing it to me. "Then he took it off and hung it in the closet because he didn't like the color. He didn't wear it long, but it's the only thing he wore that hasn't been washed."

"It'll do," I said. "We'll take it with us."

"Are you sure it will do?" she asked. I could tell she didn't think she was getting her money's worth.

"He's very good at what he does," Red assured her.

That was true. I'd like to see Mrs. Chronister try turning into a wolf.

"Why did your husband disappear?" I asked.

For a minute I thought she wasn't going to answer. Then she said, "I don't see why that matters."

"Maybe it doesn't. But you never know. Why are you afraid to tell us?"

"I'm not afraid," she said, but I could smell the fear on her.

As a matter of fact, I'd smelled it earlier, but it had been partially masked by the odor of her perfume. Poison, if it matters. She was more afraid now than she had been earlier, for some reason.

"You might as well tell us," I said. "It can't hurt, and it might even help."

She looked at Red.

"He's right," Red said. "Besides, if you don't tell us, we really can't carry this any farther. We deserve to know what we're getting into."

Mrs. Chronister slumped in her expensive chair. "It was the phone calls," she said. "He'd been getting them for weeks, but he wouldn't tell me about them. One night I listened in on an extension. A man was threatening him, telling him that he was going to kill him." She shuddered. "The voice was cold and matter of fact. I believed the man absolutely."

"And did you ask your husband about the call?" Red wanted to know.

"I did, but he wouldn't discuss it. He told me to stop worrying and leave him alone. The next day, he was gone."

"Did you tell the police about the calls?"

"No. I was afraid that if I did, the caller might come after me."

That didn't exactly follow, and I wondered if she was lying. And if she was, why. But I didn't ask. I wanted to know about Chronister's enemies.

"He didn't have any. He never hurt anyone. He was honest to a fault, and he hated lying. He couldn't abide liars."

"He sold real estate, didn't he?" I asked.

She didn't see the connection, or pretended that she didn't, and I didn't push it. The fear smell was still on her and getting stronger all the time. She was the one who was lying, but I didn't know about what.

Red asked a few more questions that didn't do much to clear things up, and we left.

"I don't trust her," I said. "She's lying."

"Maybe she's just nervous." Red didn't want to talk about it. "Can you find her husband or not?"

"If he's there, I can smell him out. But I'm not sure I want to."

"It's what we're being paid for," she reminded me.

So I told her I'd give it a shot.

I had to do it Changed. I can smell better than most humans even when I'm in their form, but for the really tough jobs I have to be a wolf.

That meant we had to wait a couple of days. Red called me twice a day, exactly the same number of times Mrs. Chronister called her, or so she said. I knew they were in a hurry, but I couldn't help that. I had to wait for the moon.

I don't know why. That's just the way it is. No one ever explained it to me. I don't know any other werewolves.

There *are* others, of course. There have to be. One of them bit my grandfather when he was in Tibet a long time ago, or so I was told. Mom always cried when she talked about it. You would too, probably, if your kid turned into a wolf the first full moon after he reached puberty. Hell, *I* cried. I was just as scared as she was. Maybe more.

Anyway, I got used to it after a while, though Mom never did. I even learned to control it. I don't *have* to Change, though it's hard to resist. And I don't kill and maim like the werewolves in movies. Give me a little steak tartare, and I'm fine.

When the first night of the full moon came, I went out into my back yard and waited. There's a seven-foot wooden fence, which is nice, since I was naked as a baby. I set a bundle of clothing on the ground and put Chronister's shirt beside it.

I could hear the stirring of the birds in the tallow tree. I could hear a rat rustling around in the woodpile near the fence. He'd better be gone before I Changed if he knew what was good for him. Rats are better than steak tartare.

The smells became stronger and stronger, the damp grass, the smoke from someone's barbecue grill, the exhaust from the cars passing on the street. I tuned them out, concentrating on Chronister's shirt.

When the moon began to edge into the darkening sky, I could feel my whole body begin to tingle. The hairs stood up on my arms and on the back of my head. I felt a powerful urge, which I withstood, to throw back my head and howl. I didn't want to scare the neighbors.

And then I Changed.

It hurts like hell. Trust me. Something happens to your bones, your skull, your hands and feet. Your eyes. Your hair. And all of it hurts. Even the hair.

But then it's over, and you're in a different world. You can't see quite as well. It's like watching TV with bad reception. But you can smell so that scents are almost like seeing. I could *smell* the rat now, as well as hear him, and I could smell more than that.

What I could see most plainly was the moon, and this time it was almost too much, but I didn't give in to the howling this time, either. Instead I grabbed Chronister's shirt and chewed it. For some reason that helped me smell it better.

Then I heard a car horn. I got rid of the shirt and grabbed up the clothing bundle. With the clothes in my mouth I ran to the gate in the fence and nosed it open.

Red's car was parked in the street with the back door swung wide. I ran across the yard and jumped in.

"My God," she said. "Is that you?"

I don't know whether she expected me to answer, but I hoped not. Wolves can't talk. Or bark, for that matter. I put the clothing in the seat and made a sort of woofing sound, which is the best a wolf can do, and that seemed to satisfy her. She reached back and closed the door and we were off.

I live in a little town about thirty minutes from downtown Houston, so while we drove I enjoyed myself. I'd never ridden in a car while I was Changed before. I stuck my head out the window and enjoyed the way the wind blew in my mouth and whipped my tongue out to the side.

"Shouldn't you hide?" Red asked.

I didn't answer, of course, but I wasn't worried. As I said, I'm sort of a mongrel, as I suppose my spiritual father must have been, and I look enough like a big dog to pass for one.

When we got near the Elevated, Red stopped the car and opened the door. I jumped out. The idea was that I'd spot Chronister, lope back to the car, Change, get into my clothing, and go after him in my human shape.

"She saw him right down the block from here," Red told me.

I woofed and started to trot away.

"Be careful," Red called.

I turned and woofed again.

The smell of the area under the Elevated was almost overpowering. Most of the people under there hadn't bathed for quite a long time, but that odor was almost masked by the pervasive scent of insect sprays of every kind. Whatever anyone had been able to find had been sprayed on with abandon.

I didn't blame them. Fleas are no picnic. Mosquitoes aren't either.

There was also the smell of gas and diesel exhaust, of hot concrete that was just now beginning to cool down from the day, of rancid hamburgers and moldy clothing and excrement and wet coffee grounds and beer and wine and cardboard and a million other things.

I loved it.

I padded along past a couple of guys talking by a box that had once held a twenty-seven-inch TV set. They didn't pay much attention to me. I have a sort of lean and hungry look; they probably thought I was after a handout. Neither of them smelled like Chronister.

I went on down, smelling my way and listening to the hundreds of cars that whirred by on the Elevated above us. No one up there had any idea of what was right below them, little old men with no teeth, black guys wearing stocking caps pulled down over their ears even in the heat, kids just barely out of their teens who hadn't had a job or a decent meal in months, winos who hadn't worked in a lot longer than that and didn't want to, and dozens of others.

A lot of them watched me out of the corners of their eyes,

and I could smell something strange mingled in with all the other scents, a mixture of fear and desire and something else I couldn't name. Anxiety? It was all wrong, and I didn't know why.

Then I smelled Chronister. He stepped out from behind a refrigerator box, and he was holding a rifle. The rifle was pointed right at me.

I caught on then, of course, just when it was almost too late.

Almost. That was the key word.

Instead of panicking or backing up or twisting to the side, which I knew would be hopeless, I charged right at Chronister. When I saw his eyes widen, I jumped.

He hadn't been expecting that, and when the rifle went off the tranquilizer dart hissed by right under me and hit someone who was following along. I heard a scream, but that was all because I struck Chronister in the middle of the chest and we went down together.

He hit hard and dropped the rifle, but he was game, I'll give him that. He tried to get a grip on me, but I twisted and thrashed and didn't give him a chance. I nipped his ear and tasted the hot squirt of his blood and then I was gone, around the refrigerator box and up Crawford Street.

The whole howling mob was right behind me. God knows what Chronister had promised them. I just hoped they weren't going to collect.

It must've made a pretty interesting sight to the few people driving by: A big, skinny dog being pursued by half the homeless population of Houston, and a few that just looked homeless. Those were Chronister's men. And women. Some in rags and some in tags and some in velvet gowns. Well, maybe no one in velvet gowns. Chronister's people would be easy to spot, however; they'd be the ones with the dart guns.

Horns honked as I cut across the traffic and went past St. Joseph's hospital. I wondered how far we'd have to go before the cops got in on the chase. I hoped it wouldn't be too far. Or I thought I did. Maybe the cops were on Chronister's side, too.

I hooked a left on Calhoun, looking for an alley to duck into. A dart hissed by my right ear and bounced off a brick wall. I wondered if it would have stopped me if it had hit me. I was more or less impervious to normal weapons; I wasn't so sure about drugs.

And that was probably why Chronister hadn't tried for me earlier. He didn't know either.

The whole thing had been a trap from the beginning, I could see that now. No wonder Mrs. Chronister had been afraid. She'd known what I was all along. And no wonder her story was so weak. She'd been ad-libbing. I should have tipped sooner. There'd been nothing about Chronister's disappearance in the papers, not that I'd seen. A guy like that doesn't drop out of sight without leaving a ripple or two.

I didn't have time to worry about it, though. I was too busy zigging and zagging to avoid tranquilizer darts.

I could easily have outdistanced the whole mob, but I didn't want to. I wanted to put a stop to this before it got ridiculous.

I could have Changed, I suppose, but that wouldn't have helped. I was too far from Red and my clothing. I had a feeling that any naked man on the streets was going to get a dart, if not something worse. I wouldn't have put it past Chronister to have a few silver bullets just in case of emergency, even though I was sure he wanted me alive, probably for one of his museums or some of his experiments in the preternatural.

I ran full out for several blocks, all the way to San Jacinto Street, where I cut back for the Elevated. There weren't many cars. Rush hour was long over, and the downtown area isn't the most popular place to be after dark.

I could hear people yelling, and one voice stood out. Chronister's, probably.

"Get him, you idiots! I've got to have him!"

Well, he wasn't going to get me, though maybe he didn't know it yet. He would before long.

I found the alley I'd been looking for and turned into it. I don't think anyone saw me, so I stopped behind a dumpster and waited.

Sure enough, everyone rushed right on by, everyone but Chronister, who was straggling along behind pretty much as I'd hoped. He hadn't looked much like a guy who kept in shape, and we'd run a long way.

When he reached the alley's mouth, I howled. Not a good howl, like I'd wanted to give when the moon came out. Just a little one, just enough to get his attention.

He stopped and looked down the alley. Meanwhile everyone in front of him kept right on running.

I whined.

"Wait a minute!" he yelled over his shoulder.

I didn't think anyone heard him. I whined again.

He took a step into the alley. "Who's there?" he asked.

He sounded a little worried, but he was still carrying his dart gun.

I scrapped my front foot against a piece of hamburger wrapper that was lying beside the dumpster, then ran down the alley into the darker shadows at the other end.

He followed, carrying the dart gun pointed in my general direction.

There was another dumpster. I went behind it and

160

Changed. It hurts just as much going the other way, but I didn't make a sound. In just a few seconds, I was nothing more than a naked man, trembling a little from my efforts.

Chronister was almost on me. I lay on the warm concrete and whimpered. "Help me. A dog . . . knocked me down."

"Where did he go?" Chronister asked.

What a stupid asshole. He didn't even want to know if I was hurt. And it didn't occur to him that I might have Changed.

While his head was swiveling around, I stood up. I grabbed the barrel of the gun and jerked it toward the sky. Then I hit Chronister as hard as I could on the point of the chin. He dropped like a stone on the concrete.

The gun came free of his hands and I found myself holding it. *Why not?* I thought, and shot him.

It's not easy to organize a homeless mob, so things were pretty much breaking up as I made my way back to Red's car. Chronister's people had realized he was gone, and they were in pretty much of a panic. They'd find him sooner or later, though he might still be asleep by the time they did. Or dead. It depended on the dosage in the darts. If he'd overdone it, it wasn't my fault.

Red didn't recognize me at first. Chronister's clothes didn't fit me very well.

"What happened?" Red asked when I got in the car. Her eyes were wide with surprise.

"I'll tell you later. Right now we need to get going."

She hesitated, watching all the confusion down the block.

"Start the car," I said.

There must have been something in my voice. She started the car.

"Don't go that way," I told her. "Turn around and get on the Gulf Freeway."

She did as I instructed and soon we were cruising in the direction of Galveston.

"Why didn't you do it yourself?" I asked finally. I was tired, and my voice cracked.

She looked straight ahead, her hands at ten and two on the wheel. "Do what?"

"Shoot me. Were you afraid the dart wouldn't work? That would have been a real mess, wouldn't it? I might have killed you. After all, I'm a werewolf."

For a minute I thought she wasn't going to answer. Then she said, "It wasn't my idea, you know."

"But you're the one who told him. It had to be you. You're the only one who knows."

"I didn't go to him," she said, as if it made a difference. "There was an article in *Texas Monthly* about famous killers, and he read about the one who tried to murder my grandmother and about what happened that night. It made him think."

"Always a dangerous thing," I said.

She ignored me. "He came to me and asked about what happened. He promised me a lot of money."

"I hope you got some of it in advance."

She almost smiled. "I did."

"What did he want with me?"

"I don't know. He knew all about werewolves, though. He was certain you existed. I think he would have found you without my help if he'd had to."

"We'll never know, will we," I said.

"No," she said. "I guess we won't."

We drove in silence for quite a while. I watched the stream of headlights coming toward us across the divider in the left lanes. I wondered where so many people could be going.

Finally Red said, "What happened to Chronister?"

"Nothing much. He should be fine. Just a little taste of his own medicine."

I looked out my window. We were passing the exit for Gulf Greyhound Park.

"Pull off on the service road," I said.

She didn't ask why. She just took the next exit.

"Stop here."

She stopped and I opened the door. "This is where I get off."

"What about me?"

"You? I've always liked you. I'm not going to rip your throat out or anything."

"And you?"

"Time for me to move on," I said.

It was true. I'd find a place somewhere that I didn't know anyone, a place where I could work and not have to deal with human beings. I'd been right about them all along; they were best avoided. I was a little disappointed, sure, but not surprised.

"Chronister will be looking for you."

"He won't find me. He won't have anyone to help him."

Red looked at me hard. "I'm sorry about that."

Maybe she even meant it, not that it made any difference.

"Sure," I said. "See you around."

I started walking across a field behind a motel. When I reached a thin stand of trees, I started taking off Chronister's clothes. I looked back. Red's car was gone.

I dropped down on all fours and Changed. The grass was damp and cool. The moon was huge and round and pale. This time, I howled. I wondered if there any lady schnauzers in the neighborhood. I hoped so.

And now, as they say, for something completely different. I usually write fairly lighthearted stories, but now and then I take a walk on the dark side. Sometimes with a vengeance. So be warned. Here's one example.

An Evening Out with Carl

The bitch was asking for it, he thought. She was *really* asking for it.

He was in one of those dance clubs that were so popular with the kids, the kind where you had to watch your step on the dance floor because if you didn't you might step on a tab of Ecstasy or one of the other hot designer drugs that had popped out of somebody's shirt pocket in the midst of a spectacular Lambada move.

Now and then you might even crunch down on a vial of crack, though that wasn't nearly so common in these places. The kids didn't go for it. They were too affluent for ghetto shit, wanted designer drugs to go along with their designer jeans. In fact, most of them didn't give a damn if you stepped on their fucking drugs. They were generally too ripped to care. Or know.

It was the kind of place Carl really liked.

He had never been to this particular one, of course. He never went twice to the same place. His peculiar inclinations made that impractical. No matter how wired the patrons were, there was always the chance they would remember something about him if he went there more than once.

Like his appearance.

He might as well have been there before, however. As far as he could tell, all those places were the same place. It was like they loaded the fucker up on a big truck and just moved it from one location in the city to another.

There were the same colored lights flashing on and off and running up and down the ceiling, the same music played so loud that it reverberated in your rib cage like someone was beating your heart with a bass drum stick, the same crowd of teenyboppers, yuppies, and middle-aged housewives shaking their asses off with every new dance cut the DJ slapped on the turntable. And the same smoke curling white and gray up there in the lights.

There was the same dance floor, no bigger than a good-sized dining table, where you had to be on the lookout at all times for flying elbows and flopping heads. It was like the management begrudged taking up valuable floor space that could be used for tables where the drinkers could sit and slurp up the over-priced drinks that contained barely enough alcohol to get a flea drunk if he could afford ten of them.

So what Carl liked wasn't the atmosphere and the conversation.

No, what he liked was the feeling of anonymity that he could achieve there. In the grotesque light, faces tended to take on odd planes and angles of shadow that made them difficult to recognize in normal illumination. There were so many people sweating and drinking and dancing and hitting on the unaccompanied women that one more strange face was hardly noticed at all.

And of course every now and then you came across someone like the bitch who was asking for it.

It was like she thought she was some vestal virgin. White top, white skirt, white shoes, even a white ribbon in her black, black hair.

She was no virgin, though. That was abundantly clear. The skirt hit her about mid-thigh, highlighting long, showgirl legs that were brown and seemed almost to glow with promise. The heels were five inches if they were one, and they pumped up the calves of those wonderful legs, not to mention the way they set up the gorgeous ass on which the skin was surely as tight as that on the head of a snare drum. And the white top was stretched over a pair of D-cups that measured forty-two inches at the bare minimum. Emphasis on the bare.

It was enough to make a man drool, especially a man like Carl.

He walked over to her table. Somehow she had one all to herself, though nearly everyone else in the place was having to share.

"Dance?" he said.

She gave him a speculative look with large dark eyes under long lashes that Carl were sure must be real.

"Sure," she said.

She had a husky voice that carried just below the level of the music and made the hairs stand up at the base of Carl's spine. She flowed up and out of the chair to take Carl's hand. With those heels, she was slightly taller than he was, but he didn't mind.

The DJ was spinning some 12-inch dance version of something by Janet Jackson, and Carl showed all his moves. They were pretty good ones, even he had to admit. Maybe not as hot as that fag shit's in *Saturday Night Fever*, but still damn good.

But they weren't as good as the woman's. She shook, slithered, bounced, and generally got with it in a way that Carl had rarely seen. In the middle of the record she seemed almost to go into a trance, her eyes half closed, her mouth slightly open, her tongue caught between small white teeth.

Definitely asking for it, Carl thought. For fucking sure.

Just like the rest of them.

He almost had to laugh aloud when he read about them in the newspapers. They always sounded like they were just coming home from a Girl Scout meeting when the "ski mask rapist" got them. Or like they had been over at their mom's house baking cookies for invalids in the nursing home.

It was all bullshit, as Carl well knew. They were all exactly like the woman in white, practically begging for someone who was man enough to give it to them.

And Carl was man enough for all of them, the eleven reported in the newspapers and the other nine who hadn't said a word about their experience. Probably, Carl thought, because they'd enjoyed the hell out of it. So had the eleven who'd squealed, of course. They were just too chickenshit to admit it.

"What's your name?" he said, as he walked her back to the table as the Janet Jackson record segued into the latest from Prince. There was a fine sheen of sweat on her brow and arms that reflected the flashing lights.

"Donna," she said. "What's yours?"

"Roger," he said. He never gave his real name. He knew what the cops were like. If she reported it, they'd ask her for the names of the men she'd danced with.

"Roger what?" she said.

"Roger Loomis. Thanks for the dance." He never danced with them more than once.

"Thank you . . . Roger," she said, sitting down at her table with feline grace.

He went back to his own table, which he was sharing with two spaced-out and horny young men who had confided that they were attending a local university on tennis scholarships. He thought their vacant eyes boded ill for the future of intercollegiate tennis, not that he gave a shit. They were the perfect table companions, their minds so much on their own dicks that they wouldn't remember him beyond the club's closing time. If they remembered even that long.

She left around one-thirty. Carl had danced with any number of other women, some of whom were begging for it almost as much as Donna, but he had already made his choice. He was a lot of things, but he wasn't fickle.

Carl waited until she was out the door. Then he followed.

She was easy to spot in the parking lot, dressed in white like that. Hell, it was like she was advertising.

She slipped into a white Toyota Celica, and Carl jumped into his anonymous navy blue Ford Escort. He could have afforded a more expensive car, but this one was best for his purposes. Who ever noticed an Escort?

Following her was a snap. She wasn't trying to hide from him. She didn't even know he was back there.

Their cars swooped down FM 1960 under the long line of lights that reflected off their hoods and tops.

Carl's car windows were tinted with plastic so as to be nearly black. He liked the feeling of driving along with the traffic, knowing that no one could see him, much less suspect what he was up to.

The other cars, he was sure, contained sleepy shift workers going home to cold suppers and warm beds, or maybe philandering businessmen who were going to creep into their suburban palaces ("Priced from the $90s to the $150s!") while praying that the wife and one point five kiddies didn't wake up screaming at them when they slipped in the door.

The drivers of the other cars gliding along in the cool blue light would think that Carl was just like them, if they thought of him at all.

But they would be very wrong.

★ ★ ★ ★ ★

Carl had known he was special since the first one.

She had been asking for it, too, and so on impulse he had followed her home. He'd just gotten back from a winter vacation to Colorado, and the ski mask was in the car. He pulled it on at the last minute before he climbed over her condo fence and tried the sliding glass door, which of course had been unlocked. So many of them were careless like that, if you could call it careless.

Begging for it, that's what Carl called it.

He remembered how it had felt, stepping into the darkness behind the curtain that covered the glass door, hearing the water running in the bathroom, knowing that she was right there, probably taking a shower, the water running down her taut, soapy skin and out the drain.

He didn't have a weapon; he never needed one. Just his hands, in gloves, of course. The gloves were in the car, too, but wearing them wasn't an impulse. He'd known that he needed to wear the gloves.

He waited by the wall and grabbed her when she came out of the bathroom, clamping his left arm around her throat, his right hand over her mouth. He could smell the powder on her skin.

He threw her on the bed, knelt on her back, and tore off his belt, tying her hands with it. Only then did he take his hand off her mouth.

"One word," he said. "One word, and I'll kill you. Understand?"

She nodded, her head against the bedspread.

His pants were around his thighs. He slipped down his underpants.

"You were asking for this," he said.

"No!" she said, shaking violently. "No!"

"Yes, goddammit!" he said, slamming his fist into her temple. "Say yes!"

For a minute she lay still, not saying anything at all. Then she said, "No."

She shouldn't have said that. If she'd only said yes, then he wouldn't have had to hit her again, and it would have been more fun for both of them.

As it was, he did have to hit her, and she lay still and didn't say anything at all, even when he was finished.

But she loved it, he knew that, because she didn't even report it to the police.

He'd done three before one of them turned him in.

Donna got onto the Loop from 1960 and then got off at Westheimer. Turned left a few blocks later and stopped in front of a huddle of expensive townhouses. They had to be expensive, in that area of town.

Carl drove on by, made a quick U-turn at the next corner, and parked in time to see Donna standing contemplatively by her car. Carl wondered what she was thinking about. Under the street light she looked almost ghostly in the white skirt, top, and shoes. The black, black hair was stirred by the late-night breeze.

Just as Carl cut his lights, Donna pushed away from her car and started toward one of the townhouses that was squeezed right between two others. She got a key out of her purse and opened the door. She went inside and the door closed behind her.

Carl waited for five minutes before he got out of the Escort. The ski mask was in the left back pocket of his jeans. The gloves were in the right.

He walked past Donna's door to a long driveway. Sure enough, the driveway led to covered parking for the residents.

It also led to the back entrances of the townhouses.

The area was lit up by a blue mercury vapor lamp on the light pole, but there was no one back there. There were just the empty cars, the light, and the shadows.

Carl stepped into a shadow and pulled on the ski mask and the gloves.

Then he went to the back door of the townhouse Donna had entered. He couldn't see a light in any of the windows, but that didn't mean anything. She was probably in the bathroom by now. That was the first place women generally went, and that was why he had waited. She wouldn't be likely to hear him come in.

It didn't bother Carl a bit that Donna had neighbors who shared her walls. Not one of the women he'd serviced had ever screamed, not after he'd warned them.

Asking for it, goddammit.

He smiled, his mouth stretching under the fabric of the mask.

He tried Donna's back door, but the knob didn't move.

Locked.

He wasn't worried. There was no deadbolt that he could see, just the cheap kind of lock that was part of the doorknob. The kind you always saw some guy slipping with a credit card in movies and on TV. The funny thing was that it really worked like that. He'd practiced on the one at his own apartment until he could slip it in ten seconds.

Donna's took him eight.

He palmed the knob and turned it slowly, pleased that it didn't make a sound. The hinges, too, were silent as the door swung inward to a dark kitchen.

Carl could make out a table and chairs. To his left was a cabinet with a sink in it, and beyond that a stove and oven. He took a step into the room and began to close the door.

Then his head exploded.

He came to in a bedroom.

He knew it was a bedroom because he was lying spread-eagled on a bed, his head turned to the left. His head blazed with pain, especially just behind and below his right ear, the ear that was next to the bed.

He tried to move, but he couldn't, not much, and he gradually became aware that his hands and feet were tied to the bed by some kind of silky fabric.

As his eyes began to focus, he saw that Donna was sitting across from him in a gold metal chair, her back to a make-up table surmounted by a lighted mirror. All the lights around the mirror were on, and he could see the make-up strewn over the table. There were blush brushes, mascara brushes, lipstick, powder, different shades of make-up base, other things Carl couldn't identify. There was also an ashtray.

Donna was sitting calmly, her right leg crossed over her left, smoking a cigarette.

"Hello, Roger," she said. "So nice of you to drop in on me."

It took Carl a second or two to figure out that she was using the name he'd given her at the club; he didn't see any reason to tell her that the name was wrong.

And then he realized that he was no longer wearing his ski mask or his gloves. He wasn't wearing anything at all.

For the first time, he felt a tinge of fear.

He ignored it. Maybe the bitch was kinky, but what the hell. Carl didn't mind a kink now and then.

"Hi, Donna," he said. "Anything for a good time, huh?"

Donna smiled. She uncrossed her legs and crushed out the cigarette. Her nails were long and red.

"Sure," she said. "Anything for a good time." She got

slowly out of the chair and walked over to the bed.

She stood where Carl could see her, hands on hips, legs spread.

"Like what you see?"

"You bet," Carl said, wishing his damn head didn't hurt so much. "You didn't have to hit me, Donna."

"Yes I did."

"You were waiting for me, though. How'd you know I'd come?"

"I hoped you would," she said. "You or someone. It's happened before."

"It has?"

"You'd be surprised." She kicked off the high heels. They thumped against the side of the bed, then dropped to the floor. "Want to see a little more?"

"A lot more," Carl said, thinking that this might not be so bad after all. Hell, she was not only asking for it, she was going to help him. Maybe she would even untie him. "I want to see all you've got."

"Oh, you will," Donna said. "I think you can count on that. Where shall I start?"

"How about untying me?" Being tied was a real problem. Carl wasn't sure that he could even get an erection if he were tied. *He* had to be the one in control. That was the best part of it, being in control, making them know that he could kill them if he wanted, that they had to obey him implicitly, do whatever he demanded.

Donna laughed huskily. "I can't untie you yet, Roger. I meant, what do you want me to take off first."

Carl looked at her bulging breasts. "Start at the top," he said.

"A wonderful idea," Donna said. "I'm sure you're going to be surprised, Roger."

174

Carl wished his head didn't hurt so much. "I don't think so," he said.

"I do," Donna said, pulling off the black, black hair and dropping it to the floor.

"Shit," Carl said. He liked long hair.

"You *were* surprised, weren't you," Donna said.

He was, he had to admit it, and he was even more surprised at the timber of Donna's voice. It was much lower, no longer husky.

He was even more surprised when Donna took of the white top and revealed a smooth, flat, muscular chest.

And when the skirt dropped to the floor, Carl saw—

"Jesus!" he screamed. "Oh Jesus, no!"

"I'm afraid so, Roger," Donna said, peeling off the jock strap and looking down at his/her rampant erection. "I'm afraid so."

Carl was crying now, sobs racking his body, the whole bed shaking.

"Don't be such a baby," Donna said. "You're going to love it."

"No!" Carl wailed. "No!"

Donna walked over to the bed, the erection jiggling, clamped a hand over Carl's mouth and kidney punched him.

Twice. Hard.

"Not another sound, Roger. You might disturb my neighbors. You understand?"

Carl understood, but he couldn't say so. He was in too much pain.

It didn't matter anyhow. Donna reached down to the floor and came up with the ski mask, then shoved it in Carl's mouth.

"That's much better," Donna said. "I believe I told you

my name was Donna. As you may have guessed, it's really Don."

He walked over to the make-up table, opened a drawer, and took something out. Carl watched with fear-crazed eyes.

Don came back to where Carl lay. There was a small bedside table, and Don laid the items he was carrying on it.

A package of condoms. A tube of K-Y jelly.

"You see, Carl? Nothing to worry about. I believe in safe sex."

Carl thrashed on the bed, jerking at the ties that held him bound until they bit into his skin, but he could do nothing more.

Don opened the package, took out a condom, slowly rolled it on. "Do be a good boy, Roger. You know you're going to like this." He picked up the tube of K-Y jelly. "You're going to like this a lot."

It was a couple of hours later when Wallace, Don's roommate, came in. Don was naked, sitting in the gold chair, smoking a long, thin cigarette.

Wallace looked at the unconscious man on the bed. There was blood smeared across his buttocks, blood on the bed covers. There was even still a little blood on Don.

"Jesus, Don," Wallace said, shaking his head. "This is the worst one yet."

Don didn't say anything. He blew a thin stream of smoke through his red lips.

"He'll yell for the cops," Wallace said. "He's bound to."

"No he won't," Don said. "No one's done that yet. He's just like them. Maybe worse. He'll be much too ashamed."

"Maybe," Wallace said. "But I'm not taking any more chances with you, Don. I told you what would happen if you did this again. I'm leaving."

He went into the other bedroom. Don didn't try to stop him. Later he came back, carrying two heavy leather bags. "I just don't understand, Don. I just don't understand why you do these things."

Don extended the cigarette he was smoking over the ashtray and tapped it with a long red nail. He sighed. He was tired of the argument already.

"The bitch was asking for it," he said.

This story isn't quite as dark as the previous tale, but it's no walk in the park. It's a quirky little number that I've always had a sneaking affection for. After reading it, you may never think about ties in the same way again.

Blest Be the Ties

I haven't slept for quite a long time now, almost forty-eight hours. There are several reasons why.

For one thing, I am making a catalog of Harold's ties. Harold was my husband, and for twenty-five years he received a tie from me on Father's Day. And he also received ties from our son and daughter. I bought the ties when the children were young, but they always helped me to pick them out. Later, they bought the ties themselves.

I do not believe that we were unusual in giving ties for Father's Day. I read somewhere just the other day that every year there are 12,000 miles of ties given as Father's Day gifts. Or perhaps it was 120,000 miles. I am not sure, not being very good at recalling figures, but it was one of those numbers. It definitely had something to do with *twelve;* at any rate, it represented a lot of ties.

Harold used to say that the giving of ties represented a lack of imagination. "And the kids are no better than you are. They don't have an original bone in their bodies."

That was perhaps true, but the ties represented to me (and to the children, I am sure) much more than just a gift. They were symbolic; they were the ties that bound us together in love, for all of us loved one another very much. Does such a thought show a lack of imagination? I do not think so, but I never mentioned that to Harold.

"Maybe they aren't original in their giving," I would always answer, "but they're fine children all the same."

He had to agree with that, and he did save all the ties. They hang on special racks that he built in the walk-in closet in our bedroom.

I am cataloging those on the rack that date back to the middle 1970s now. The tie I am looking at is really quite nice. I gave it to Harold myself. It is three and three-quarters of an inch wide at its widest point and has a dark brown background, with large white and blue flowers printed on it. It is a Wemlon tie, by Wembley. Here is what the label says:

CRUSH IT . . . KNOT IT . . . EVEN WASH IT . . .
FOR BROWN, GREEN OR BLACK SUIT
100% POLYESTER

Some might think that the murders are the reason I have not slept. You have probably read about the murders. Four young women have been killed within the last two months, all of them within a few miles of where I sit, but I am not worried that I will become another victim.

For one thing, I am no longer what most people think of as "young." I am fifty-five years old, which, while it might not be called young by some people, is not exactly old, either. Not these days. People are living longer all the time. I read an article not so very long ago that said the fastest growing population group in this country is composed of people from eighty to eighty-five years of age. So fifty-five isn't as old as it used to be.

Of course Harold could not see it that way, not recently at any rate. He had become fascinated with women who were twenty years younger than I. Even thirty years younger. I watched him poring over his *Playboy* every month, as if trying to discover a blemish on the perfectly smooth peach-colored skin of the Playmate of the Month.

"Harold," I always said, "those girls are young enough to be your daughter."

He would look up guiltily. "I'm just reading the interview."

I never believed him, however. It wasn't so long ago that he began asking me to call him "Harry." He seemed to think it sounded younger than "Harold," perhaps more sporty, but I refused to change. He had been Harold to me ever since we met, more than thirty years ago. Fifty-five might not be old, but it is too old to begin changing the habits of more than half a lifetime. So I did not call him Harry, and now he will always be Harold. That is the name engraved on his stone.

In addition to being fifty-five years of age, I am not of the correct physical dimensions to attract the killer, whose victims are all short and slim, as well as young, much like the Playmates of the Month. I am admittedly somewhat larger than they. I am six feet tall and weigh one hundred and seventy-six pounds. I am not fat, however. Statuesque is the term I prefer. I am quite strong and believe that I could give quite a good account of myself if I were attacked.

"Have you ever thought of joining a health club?" Harold asked me one day as he was looking through the sports section of the paper.

He had never cared for sports, and I knew perfectly well what he was looking at. He was certainly not reading the box scores from the previous night's baseball games, or even the advertisements for health clubs. He was looking at the advertisements for the "gentlemen's clubs" that advertise prime rib specials for under four dollars and feature entertainers with names like "Brenda Boobs," who are fresh from their careers in "XXX Rated Hits." I have seen the advertisements.

I asked what he meant about my joining a health club, though I thought I knew.

"Get a little exercise," he said. "Do you good. Tighten you up a little."

He himself had recently begun exercising every morning with something called a "Tummycizer," which purported to be a device that would reduce his waistline by several inches within a month. So far as I could tell, it had not yet had any effect.

The tie I am looking at now came, according to the label, from "Sears—The Men's Store." It is four and one-quarter inches wide and is 100% polyester. It is dark green, and the scene repeatedly depicted on it is that of a decaying forest, with falling brown and yellow leaves, grey stumps of trees, and four mushrooms with brown tops. The label does not instruct the wearer as to the color of suit that would be appropriate.

Harold and I were married for twenty-seven years. In all that time, I do not believe he was unfaithful to me even once; that is, not until near the end. Then it was a different story, though not a very original one.

He was two years older than I and I believed that he had successfully avoided the "midlife crisis" that I had read about so often in *Reader's Digest* and other publications. He had not, however. He had only delayed it a bit longer than most, and it struck him hard when it finally arrived.

He was, naturally enough, humiliated when I caught him out in one of his clumsy lies and told him that I knew about what was going on.

It is possible that his humiliation only increased when he later told his intentions to the young woman (I believe that she could have been no older than thirty) with whom he was currently involved. Now that I knew all, he explained to her, he would divorce me and marry her. Though it would be a struggle, since it was possible that he would soon be out of work and since no doubt the divorce would strip him of a considerable portion of his assets, he was certain that they would be happy because of the love they had for one another.

She laughed at him, of course.

She did not love Harold and was not interested in marriage with a fifty-six-year-old man, grown slightly bald, sporting a paunch that the Tummycizer had not reduced, and having no prospects for a decent income. She had gone out with him, let him pay for her meals, and accepted his gifts of money and clothing. She had probably even given him sex as a reward (though he never admitted that to me), but she was not in the least interested in marrying him. So her reaction to his declaration was predictable. Had Harold asked me (as of course he did not), I could have told him what she would do. I might have done the same thing myself at her age and in similar circumstances had I ever been involved in anything so sordid as an extra-marital affair, which of course I never was.

I could never have told Harold, however, how he himself would react. I would never have expected it, and I am sure that he did not expect it either.

At home, Harold had always been mild. Not meek, exactly, but certainly mild. He never raised his voice to the children when they were growing up, not even on the day that Dwayne put the cat into his wagon and rolled it into the street in front of the oncoming traffic.

This time was quite different, I suppose because Harold had been under a great deal of pressure at home (from me) and at work. The job that he had held for nearly thirty years was being eliminated, and while the company had a private pension plan, it was not a very good one. Too, it did not go into effect until the worker reached the age of sixty-two. Add to all that the crisis of masculinity (or whatever it was) that Harold was experiencing, and the stress must have been considerable.

Not that I am trying to excuse him. He should never have done what he did, and I can never hope really to understand why it happened. There are no doubt circumstances besides those I have cited and that I do not know about. I can never know them now.

What Harold did was to kill the young woman and dump her in a ditch on a deserted section of a county road that branched off Highway 288. She was found shortly thereafter, becoming the first in the series of victims that I referred to above.

I am looking now at an Arrow tie, four and one-quarter inches wide. It is brown, with three narrow diagonal white stripes crossing it near the bottom. It is, like the others from this rack, made of one hundred percent polyester. It is not, of course, the tie that Harold used to strangle the young woman. Ties these days are much narrower, though perhaps they are still made of polyester. I have not come to the newer ties as yet. They are on another rack.

"Why, Harold?" I asked him, when he came home and confessed everything to me.

He had his own little apartment by that time, but I am sure he felt a need to talk to someone, and he knew that I could never turn him away. I had not even wanted him to go in the first place. I had never been comfortable without him in the house, and I would have tied him to me if I could have. Leaving was his idea, not mine.

At any rate, that night he came home. He tried to explain himself, I suppose, but he was unable to do so.

"Because," he said. "Because. . . ."

But that was all he could say. He was sobbing and incoherent, and I told him to get undressed and go to bed. I told him that everything would be all right, though of course it would not. How could it be?

I was hoping, however, that what had happened might bring him back to me. As far as I was concerned, the woman who had almost succeeded (though perhaps that had never been her intention) in breaking up my home was dead. She had received no more than she deserved. Justice was served, Harold's fling was over, and he was at home where he belonged. I gave him a pill to help him sleep, but I am not sure that he took it. Most likely he did not.

I went to the closet at that time and looked at all the ties. He had taken only a few of them with him to the apartment, but I was glad that he had taken them. I had felt that somehow they would bring him back to me, and I suppose that they did, if hardly in the way I had expected.

I am sure that I know which one he used. It was one of his favorites, the one that Dwayne gave him last year. It had a gaudy floral pattern, but I do not recall the name of the manufacturer.

Harold died sometime very early the next morning, somewhere between four and five o'clock. I was sleeping in another room, and while I cannot be sure that he was sleeping as well, I hope that he was. That would make his death at least a little easier to bear. I would hate to think that he lay awake torturing himself by agonizing over that woman, who so richly deserved her end.

But because I was not with him, I cannot really be sure of the time of death, only that it must have been between four and five o'clock. That is what the doctor estimated.

His heart had not been strong for several years. The doctors repeatedly had warned him about his blood pressure and his cholesterol count, both of which were elevated. They had even told him to stop smoking, and he had done so for a while. Recently, however, probably because of the stress, he had started again. I had spoken to him about it, but to no avail.

So the young woman—the young *women,* as I am sure there had been more than one even though he never admitted as much—took Harold away from me a second time. Permanently. The ties did not bind, not forever.

The funeral was distressing, to both me and the children, who loved their father almost as much as I. I did not tell them of their father's infidelities. It would have done no good at all and might have done much harm. Nor did I mention the death of the young woman. I did not want to upset them needlessly. It was right for them to remember their father as he had every right to be remembered.

I have passed the time since Harold's death in various ways. I read the newspapers thoroughly every day. I watch television. Recently I have begun to catalogue the ties, and each one reminds me of what a good husband and father Harold was until very near the end of his too-short life.

The tie I have here now, for example, is particularly nice. It has a geometric pattern of browns, blues, and blacks. It was designed by Oleg Cassini, whose name, I believe, is highly respected in the world of fashion, though oddly enough the tie was made in Burma. That seems a strange place for a tie to have been made, and surely Oleg Cassini is not a Burmese name.

The young women continue to die, all of them strangled with ties, which also seems strange. They are very careless it appears, leaving their "gentlemen's clubs" unescorted at all hours of the night, prey for anyone clever enough to await them at the right place or stupid enough to allow themselves to be lulled by someone they do not expect to kill them.

Harold is not the killer. He did kill the first one, as I have explained, but he can kill no more. I am not sure that I know who killed the others.

I do know, however, that I have dreams, strange dreams. In some of them I am waiting in lighted parking lots, looking lost and distracted, as if I need assistance. Young women ask if they can help, and I ask them for a ride. I do not remember what happens after that, though I have tried.

There are no female serial killers, or very few. I read that in an article not so long ago. The article mentioned that there was one woman who, I believe, posed as a hitchhiker and killed a number of men, but there have been no other women that I am aware of who have done so.

The dreams trouble me, however, and that is why I prefer to remain awake. If I do not sleep, then I cannot dream. And if the dreams are more than dreams, then what have I become?

That is why I am cataloging the ties. There seem to be fewer of them now than there were when Harold died. But there are so many. It is hard to be sure.

Next time, I will know. I will have the list that I am working on, and I can check to be certain. If one is missing, then I will know. I do not know what I will do then.

But that is then, and this is now. Now I believe that I will have a cup of coffee, very strong coffee. And then I will work on my catalog of ties again, beginning with that bright orange one there. Not quite as wide as the others, but certainly from the same time period.

The 1970s were a very colorful era, and Harold was a man who liked color. He particularly liked that orange tie, which Dwayne gave him for Father's Day. He swung Dwayne into the air and said, "Blessed be the ties that bind, right, Dwayne?"

Dwayne laughed and laughed, and Harold put him down, winking at me. I wonder if he somehow knew what I secretly thought about the ties. I wonder whether the ties bind us even now, but if they do, it is in a way that I do not care to think about any longer.

I will make the coffee especially strong.

And then I will look at the ties.

Elvis and vampires? As with the werewolf detective, I ask, why not?

King of the Night

For as long as he could remember, Elvis had been a creature of the night.

Maybe it had started back in the early days when he was recording for Sam Phillips at Sun and touring in the car with Bill and Scotty, driving to the gig (most likely some high school hop), playing till after midnight, driving home again, and getting to sleep about the time the sun came up. Even then he'd liked the way the world looked and smelled at night better than the day.

He'd gotten on a different schedule in the Army, of course, and when he'd been making movies he'd had to live pretty much like everyone else except that he got up earlier, but during the Vegas years he'd gotten back into the habit of sleeping during the day and living his life after dark. It was easier that way, easier to avoid the crowds and easier to avoid the people who wanted something from him, which at times seemed to include just about everyone from the Colonel on down.

Finally the nightlife began to seem like the only life, and for him the nighttime was the right time. It was the only time.

He sat up in bed and looked at the digital clock radio on the nightstand. The green numerals read 6:33. Outside the cheap motel room, the sun was going down. He tossed back the sheet and sat up. Time to be thinking about breakfast.

After he shaved and dressed, he sat down in the uncomfortable vinyl-covered chair at the round table by the window. Then he put on his bifocals and flipped through the copy of the *Weekly World News* he'd picked up at a convenience store the previous evening. He bought one every now and then to see what they were saying about him, to see if he was speaking from beyond the grave with "a special message for Lisa Marie" or whether he was going to be singing in some Baptist choir on Easter Sunday morning.

This time the article claimed that within the year he would do a live performance of a song written by a reader of the *Weekly World News*. Several sample songs were printed on the page, and there was a big photo of himself. He didn't look like that anymore. He looked a lot like his daddy had, kind of skinny and mean. Giving up drugs and deep-fried peanut-butter-and-banana sandwiches really changed a man. That, and developing a severe case of male pattern baldness.

He gave the songs only a cursory glance. He wasn't really interested in music these days except for the old songs. About the only singing he did was in the shower, and he never listened to the radio anymore, not since all you could hear was that rap shit, which he couldn't follow at all. He couldn't understand the words.

What really interested him wasn't the article about himself, anyway. His eye had been caught by an ad on another page, offering something called Count Dracula's Pendant, filled with earth from the Count's birthplace in Transylvania. Only $39.95, shipping and handling included. There was a dragon emblem on the front, and Elvis thought it would have looked pretty good on his white jumpsuit back in the old days, not that he needed to carry around earth from Dracula's birthplace. But it was an interesting idea. It might explain a thing or two.

He closed the paper, tossed it in the trash, and looked outside again. For a minute or so he watched the cars passing up

190

and down Telephone Road. It was completely dark now, or as dark as it ever got in Houston, what with all the streetlights and the stores and the billboards. It was time to go looking for the one who called himself The King.

He'd seen him first in Memphis, late one night after buying all the tickets for a movie so that he and the Memphis Mafia could have the theater to themselves.

The man came in just as the movie was over and stood in the back of the theater, looking as if he thought he had a right to be there. One of the crew braced him of course. You didn't fuck around with Elvis. Too many people wanted to prove their loyalty or their manhood or something. It was Red, Elvis thought, who stood up this time.

He could remember the conversation that echoed in the theater.

"What the hell are you doin' in here, buddy?" Red asked. "Don't you know this is a private party?"

"I wasn't aware that it was a party at all," the man said. His voice was cold and hollow. "I just wanted to see The King."

"Well, he don't want to see you."

Elvis remembered the man perfectly. He was tall, probably six-one, and pale. His eyes were red, like a cat's eyes after dark. His hair was jet black, and Elvis was impressed. Here was a guy who knew how hair should look. It was too bad that 'Cilla never caught on. Elvis had seen her on TV not long ago, and her hair was almost blond.

"He might want to see me," the man said. "After all, he is using my name."

"What, is your name Elvis?" Red glanced back over his shoulder to see if the Mafia appreciated his wit.

The man smiled. "No. It is the other name I mean. I am

191

The King. The King of the night."

"Like hell you are." Red put a hand to the man's chest and shoved, but the man didn't even budge.

"There is no need to be rude," he said, looking right straight at Elvis, and the next thing Elvis knew Red was tumbling down the aisle, ass over elbows. The guy had hardly even moved, and before anyone else could jump him, he was gone.

That got everybody hot under the collar, and two or three of them tried to borrow Elvis' gun. He'd been carrying a Smith & Wesson .357 Magnum revolver that night, but he knew it wouldn't do them any good.

"Never mind, fellas," he said. "Let's us go on home."

Naturally that's what they did, since Elvis had suggested it. Nobody ever gave him any back talk.

When they got back to Graceland, everybody wanted to do something different—play handball, shoot pool, swim—but Elvis just went to his bedroom. He had to think about what he'd seen, which he was pretty sure was a vampire. He'd dealt with enough bloodsuckers in his career, from the Colonel on down, to recognize another one when he saw him.

He turned on the TV to help him think, but there was Robert Goulet in some rerun from *The Carol Burnett Show*, singing a stupid song from *Camelot*. Elvis pulled out his Magnum and shot out the picture tube, which spouted sparks and blue smoke as it exploded with a noise even louder than the gunshot.

Nobody came to see what had happened. Either they were used to it (it was the second TV he'd shot in less than a month—the last time had been because of Mel Torme) or they so were intent on what they were doing downstairs that they didn't hear. Elvis didn't care one way or the other. He was tired of trying to explain what pissed him off so much about Robert Goulet.

It wasn't really his singing so much as the fact that he was married to Carol Lawrence, who, it seemed to Elvis, should have been married to *Steve* Lawrence, which would have made sense, but Steve Lawrence was married to Edie Gorme, whose last name sounded a lot like Goulet. Carol and Steve Lawrence. Robert and Edie Goulet. Or Gorme. Just thinking about it pissed him off. He started to shoot out one of the other TVs in the room just for the hell of it, but he restrained himself.

Then he thought of another reason why he didn't like Robert Goulet. Goulet looked a lot like the vampire.

The vampire killed a woman that night; Elvis read about it in the paper the next day: "Woman's Body Drained of Blood," the headline said, and there were fears of a serial killer stalking the city.

It didn't work out like that, however. There were no more deaths by blood draining, at least not in Memphis, but over the next few years it happened several times in different places. No one noticed, except Elvis, as he thought the vampire expected him to.

The vampire was obsessed with being The King.

Elvis wasn't all that surprised. It was the sort of thing that had happened to him before. Never with a vampire as far as he knew, but people were always identifying with him in some weird way, following him, hanging around the mansion, wanting to be him, thinking that in some freaky way they *were* him. Hell, even Jerry Lee Lewis had tried to climb the fence at Graceland once.

But the vampire was something entirely different, which made it interesting, and there was damn little that was interesting to Elvis in those days. He had more money than he'd ever dreamed of, he'd swiveled his hips on stage and made women cry with desire, he'd been a movie star (though there were a couple of those movies he wished he'd never made, especially *Kissin' Cousins*), he'd starred in Vegas and on TV, he'd had every woman he'd ever wanted (not to mention a few he didn't). But finally he'd gotten tired of all of it. There wasn't a thing that didn't bore him stiff, and so, sure, he did a few drugs. And he ate. Blew up like a goddamn blimp. Shit, Macy's was thinking about hiring him to be a balloon in their next Thanksgiving Day parade.

He knew he had to do something, that he was killing himself, but he just didn't care. The last time he'd had any fun was in what people were calling his "comeback special" on TV in 1969. He'd liked that because he was doing what he did best, playing his guitar in front of a small crowd that appreciated what they were hearing. If he could've kept doing that, he might've been happy.

But he couldn't keep doing it. He was Elvis, and Elvis played only the biggest and the best venues in front of thousands of people; he didn't perform in little places where probably less than a hundred people were crowded into the tight space around him. The Colonel would never have let him get away with it. So there was nothing to do except eat and take pills, and there was no way he could pull himself out of the nosedive he was taking, not until he got interested in the vampire.

Hell, *somebody* had to stop him.

There was a Denny's on I-45, and Elvis drove there in the dilapidated Cadillac he'd been using for several years now. It wasn't pink; he couldn't take a chance on that, even looking like he did. Somebody just might make the right connection, not that it would really matter. The tabloids would just write up another Elvis sighting and everyone would think it was just another story by another demented fan.

The Caddy was gray, and he didn't like it nearly as much as the first one he'd ever bought, but it was reliable. It had been hauling him around the country for more than ten years now, and it got him to Denny's.

He didn't eat much, just a couple of eggs over easy with sausage and toast. No one in the place paid the least attention to him. He did nothing to call attention to himself, and he appeared to be just an ordinary-looking man, a little past middle age, with dyed hair, a growing bald spot, and bifocal glasses with cheap plastic frames.

He was wearing a faded denim jacket over a white cotton shirt and Levis that were faded to nearly the color of the shirt. He might have been a long-haul trucker or maybe a shift worker at one of the chemical plants in Pasadena or Texas City.

As he chewed the sausage, he thought about the conversation he'd had with Red the day after the vampire had come into the theater.

"Vampire? Are you shittin' me, E?"

"No, man. I think that's what we saw last night."

"C'mon, E. You know better'n that. There ain't no such thing as a vampire. You been watchin' too many of those horror movies on TV."

Elvis said he'd seen some horrible things on TV, all right, but that they weren't about vampires.

"I want to know some more about them things," he said. "Who can I talk to?"

Since Elvis seemed to be serious, Red gave it some thought. "You might talk to Sam. He reads a lot of junk, like about vampires and things."

"Get him," Elvis said, and Red did.

It turned out that Sam knew plenty. He told Elvis about the Undead and how they preyed on the living, sucking their blood and robbing them of life to sustain their own foul existence.

"They sound like bad sonsabitches," Elvis said.

"They're bad, sure enough," Sam said.

Elvis grinned. "Not any worse than a lot of live people I know, though."

Sam knew a little about Elvis' financial arrangements, and he knew all about 'Cilla and how she cheated on E. with her karate instructor. "You could be right about that, E."

"How do you kill 'em? With a wooden stake like in the movies?"

Sam nodded. "Or cut off their heads. Do both is supposed to be best. Stake 'em and cut off their heads too."

"I think I could do that," Elvis said, and Sam couldn't tell whether he was talking about doing it to vampires or somebody else, like 'Cilla's karate teacher, but he didn't ask.

Outside the Denny's Elvis took a deep breath of the Houston air, which smelled like exhaust fumes and fried food and hot concrete and chemical stink, with just a little bit of salt air from the Gulf thrown in. The cars and trucks swooshing by on the Interstate were a constant stream of headlights going one way and taillights the other.

Elvis wasn't far from Hobby Airport, and he wondered if the vampire knew he was there. Probably. The sonofabitch was pretty damn smart. He'd been eluding Elvis for more than fifteen years now, ever since Elvis had staged his own death. Compared to catching a vampire, that part had been easy. Stuff like that was always easy if you had the money, and Elvis had plenty of that. Even after fifteen years he still had plenty of that; there was an old suitcase full of it in the trunk of the Caddy.

He'd decided to fake his death after he read about the vampire's fourth killing. Elvis didn't think they all made the papers, so it was probably more than four all together, but enough of them got reported so that you could see there was a pattern to them, if you were looking for it.

Elvis didn't even really have to look. He'd figured it out by the second killing. It was like he'd known all along, but it took two more before he decided to do something about it.

"A million dollars?" the doctor had said. "I can't take that much, Elvis. You're a friend."

"You'll earn it," Elvis told him. "You're gonna have to take a lotta heat from the papers and all. And you're gonna have to find a body for the box. One that looks a little like me 'ud be best. You know one of them papers'll try to get a pi'ture. I 'magine you'll have to pay off a few people at the funeral home, too."

"What about your girlfriend?"

Elvis had been worrying about her. He always had to have a woman around to keep up appearances, though to tell the truth he just wasn't that interested in women anymore. They were like everything else—boring, mostly.

Even at that he didn't want to make this one feel too bad, but he didn't see any help for it. "I can fake her out. I been in enough bad movies to act dead."

"Why're you doing this, Elvis? I just don't understand it. You've got everything a man could want."

"Not ever'thing," Elvis said.

"What then? If you don't have it, it can't be anything a normal man would want."

"Sure it is. It's what ever'body wants."

The doctor frowned and shook his head. "I don't know what that could be."

"A reason," Elvis said.

"What kind of a reason?"

"A reason to give a damn."

The doctor shook his head again, but he didn't try to argue anymore. He said he'd take the money.

Elvis drove the Caddy to the motel near the airport where the lighted sign announced that the "Elvis Impersonator Contest" was being held.

The impersonations were something that Elvis figured was a natural outgrowth of people thinking they wanted to be him. They'd started in a small way before he "died," and a guy named Ral Donner had even had a couple of big hit records back in the fifties by managing to sound just like Elvis, but Elvis had figured that by now nobody would be interested anymore.

It hadn't worked like that, though. There was more interest now than ever, and if tonight was like most of the other nights the contest would have plenty of Elvises: overweight Elvises, young Elvises, oriental Elvises, child Elvises, probably some south-of-the-border Elvises, and even a female Elvis or two. They would all have one thing in common. Not a one of them would be able to sing a lick.

That was the worst part, having to listen to them and having to watch them try to make the moves that were right only when you didn't have to try, and sometimes it was almost enough to make Elvis want to stand up out of his seat, walk up to the stage, give his shoulders a shake or two, and wail out a few lines of "That's All Right" or maybe "Mystery Train" just to show them how it was done.

But he never did. He couldn't break his cover. There was

198

always the chance that the vampire would be there. Sam had told him that they were shape-changers.

"They can be animals if they want to," Sam had said. "Not just bats. Wolves, too. Things like that."

Elvis thought that was a good talent to have. A man that could be a wolf wouldn't have to go around renting a whole amusement park just to get a little privacy. "What about different kinds of people?"

Sam thought about it and decided he didn't see why not. "If you can look like a wolf, you can look like just about anybody you damn well please."

Maybe you couldn't look *exactly* like anybody you damn well pleased, though, Elvis thought. But you could probably get close enough.

So he started getting the papers from every town where there was some kind of Elvis impersonator contest. And sure enough, now and then there would be a story about a spooky murder that had happened in the same city. The murders weren't always the same, and that was before the cops got all their computers together, so no one really noticed. No one except Elvis. He knew what was going on.

He parked the Caddy and got out. Looked like there would be a pretty good crowd. You could never tell about these things, though. He should know. He'd been to enough of them.

He'd never caught up with the vampire, though, not quite. In the first place, the vampire didn't go to every single contest, probably no more than one a year. Elvis figured that was done on purpose to keep the cops from seeing a pattern in the killings.

And when the vampire did get into a contest, it might not be the one where Elvis was. There was no way to predict his movements, so if Elvis was at a performance in Chicago, the vampire might be on stage in Reno. If Elvis was in Shreve-port, the vampire would be in Denver. Elvis could track him only after the fact by the stories in the papers, the stories of the deaths of transients or waitresses or bank managers or anyone who fell in the vampire's way.

Once or twice their paths had crossed. There had been that time in Dallas, and another time in Atlanta. The vampire always used different names to enter the contests, and he always looked different, but Elvis knew he had been there. He just couldn't tell which of the fakes was the vampire, and the vampire didn't give himself away, not until the story in the paper the next day or the day after that.

But this time was going to be different. Elvis just had a feeling about that.

The cover charge wasn't much, and while there was a pretty good crowd, Elvis didn't have any trouble getting a table close to the tiny stage.

The announcer was a guy with a desperate smile and a rug that made him look like a ferret had died on his head. He tried to work up some enthusiasm in the audience with a series of bad jokes, but he wasn't having much luck.

"Yessir," the man said, "I don't know about you, but I ate dinner right here in our very own restaurant. No wonder they call this place Heartburn Hotel."

There was a half-hearted rimshot from the drummer of the three-piece combo that was set up to accompany the imper-sonators, but Elvis was the only one who laughed. He'd al-ways liked that joke; he'd used it often enough himself.

"Hey, folks, these are the jokes. Don't put me in a mystery strain!"

Rimshot, then silence, except for Elvis' brief guffaw.

"Well, people, you gotta admit I take a lickin' and keep on

tickin'. It's like the gasoline said to the car, 'Now and then there's a fuel such as I.' "

Another rimshot, another laugh from Elvis, another round of silence from the fans.

"OK, OK, I get the picture. You want some Elvis. Well, all right. Whoops, that's a Buddy Holly song!"

No laughter, not even from Elvis.

"Never mind, never mind. You people must have wooden hearts. Let's get the real show started. First up tonight is a man who calls himself Johnny Tender. Let's have a big hand for him as he sings 'Lovin' You'!"

There wasn't much of a hand, but then Johnny Tender didn't deserve one, not to Elvis' way of thinking. He butchered the song, his hair was combed bad, and it wasn't even black. He moved like an eighty-year-old with fleas.

The next three weren't much better. They tried, but that was about all you could say for them.

Then came number five. He called himself The King, and Elvis knew he had his man.

The King had brought his own music, provided by a portable Bose Acoustic Wave Machine and a CD that played the theme from 2001. He was wearing a white jumpsuit and a heavy white cape that he swirled dramatically as he jumped up on the stage. His face was just a little puffy, and he had a red scarf around his neck.

The tape segued from "2001" into "Viva Las Vegas," and he began teasing the crowd, swiveling his hips woodenly and swinging the mike on its cord. A couple of women screamed.

"Elvis!" someone yelled. "It's him! It's really him!"

It was enough to make the real Elvis sick to his stomach. And then the vampire started to sing.

Elvis' mouth fell open. Holy shit. The vampire sounded just like Robert Goulet.

201

The crowd didn't notice. They were completely taken in. It was probably the jump suit, Elvis thought.

The vampire concluded, holding the slightly flat final note on "Las Vegaaaaaaaaaaaaaassssssssssss" interminably, setting Elvis' teeth on edge while slipping one scarf after another from around his neck and giving them to the women who came up with outstretched hands. There must've been twenty of them.

Then the vampire was gone, taking his music machine with him and disappearing down a corridor back of the stage. Elvis went after him, the applause fading behind him.

There was a door at the end of the corridor and Elvis saw it closing. Then he heard it click firmly shut. He broke into a run.

The door led into the parking lot, and the vampire was standing there under the blue glow from the mercury vapor lamps high on their silver poles.

The light made everything look strange and Elvis thought that he and the vampire might probably look like they were standing under the blue moon of Kentucky. The Bose was sitting on the pavement nearby, not far from the Caddy that Elvis had arrived in.

The vampire stared calmly at Elvis. He didn't look a thing like he had looked inside the hotel. Maybe it was the lights, but he looked older and more evil, though the jumpsuit still looked sharp.

"I was very good, wasn't I?" he said.

Elvis looked him up and down. "Hell no. You were awful. You sounded like Robert Goulet."

"They loved me!"

"They loved the way you looked. The jumpsuit ain't bad. The rest is bullshit."

The vampire's eyes flashed red. "You lie."

"You're the liar," Elvis said. "Tryin' to be somethin' you're not. You can't sing. You can't move. Why don't you give it up?"

"You wouldn't understand," the vampire said.

Elvis shrugged. "Try me."

The vampire sighed theatrically. "You humans are so limited. But very well. Imagine you have lived for a thousand years. Impossible, no?"

"No," Elvis said. Sometimes he thought he'd lived a lot longer than that; he'd just done it in a lot less time. "I can imagine that pretty easy."

The vampire looked as if he didn't believe it, but he went on. "Very well. In a thousand years one sees many things. Does many things. But after so long a time, these things begin to pall. Life grows drab and monotonous."

Elvis nodded. He knew exactly what the vampire was talking about.

"And so one needs something to keep him going, something to add a bit of . . . piquancy, shall we say, to his life. Do you understand me?"

"Yeah. Prob'ly a lot better'n you think."

"So I became intrigued with you, the man they called The King. Because, you see, I believe that *I* am The King. The King of the Night. I rule the darkness in ways that you do not, cannot, understand."

"I read the papers," Elvis said.

"That part is not like you think. It gives me no pleasure. It is simply that I must have their blood to live. They sustain me. And they feel no pain."

"I bet they don't."

"But that is beside the point. The point is that I wanted to see what it meant to have the kind of power that you have. You can command awe; so can I, but it is an awe based in fear. But you command love, adoration. I wanted to feel that kind of power."

"If you feel it, it's just because you're an imitation of me, and a damn poor one at that."

The vampire's lips pulled back from his teeth. Elvis saw the sharp incisors, hollow so they could drain the blood.

"That may be true," the vampire said. "But there is another way for me to become you, at least for a short time. Why do you think I let you find me tonight, tonight after all these years?"

"You're tired of runnin' around the country makin' a fool of yourself and soundin' like Robert Goulet?"

"You are not funny," the vampire said. "But that does not matter. Soon you will be a part of me, and I will become a part of you."

"I thought you might have somethin' like that in mind," Elvis said. He pulled his .357 from inside the denim jacket and let the light from one of the lamps fall on the chrome-plated barrel.

The vampire sneered. Elvis wasn't impressed. He could do better.

"Now I will show you my power," the vampire said, taking a step toward Elvis.

"That's a nice medallion you've got," Elvis said, gesturing with the pistol barrel.

The vampire's hand went to his throat. A thick gold medallion about the size of saucer hung there from a heavy gold chain.

Elvis pulled the trigger.

The bullet went right through the vampire's hand, and the medallion exploded, almost like a TV screen, and dirt flew everywhere. The bullet veered off and went through the vampire's shoulder and out the back. The vampire wasn't bothered.

"You better gather all that dirt up," Elvis said. "Else you won't have any place to sleep tomorrow."

"You fool," the vampire said. "I have other soil that I can reach before sunrise. Your bullets will not stop me."

"I wouldn't count on that if I was you," Elvis said, and he pulled the trigger again.

This time the bullet slammed into the vampire's chest and stayed there. The vampire jerked erect and shrieked with pain and fear. His face twisted as he sank to his knees; his hands clutched at his heart.

"Wooden bullets," Elvis said. "I thought of 'em myself. Looks like they're workin'." The vampire moaned and toppled over on his side. "I don't guess I'll have to cut off your head after all."

The vampire was rotting away right there in the parking lot. He opened his moldering mouth and said, "*I* am . . . The King."

"You're not much of anything," Elvis said. "Just a pile of dust."

And before long, that's all he was.

Elvis didn't watch the whole transformation, however. He didn't want to stick around the parking lot too long. Even in Houston, someone was bound to call the cops about those gunshots. He walked over and picked up the Acoustic Wave Machine and went back to the hotel.

The last impersonator, a pimply fifteen-year-old, had just finished butchering "Teddy Bear" when Elvis sat back down at his table. There was scattered applause, but not much. Elvis felt seriously depressed and a whole lot older than the vampire had been.

Hell, he never should've killed him. The vampire was what had kept him going for fifteen years. What the hell was he

205

going to do with the rest of his life? It wasn't like he could call up the Colonel and say, "Hey, I'm back."

The announcer came out onto the stage. "All right, folks, that's it for the night, unless there's some hunka hunka burnin' love right here in the audience who thinks they can do better. What about it? Anybody here who wants to get up on the stage and show us what they've got? Remember, the prize is two hundred and fifty dollars." He paused for a minute, looking out at the audience. "No takers? Well, we'll have to vote on the winner then."

Elvis heard people at the other tables talking among themselves. It was no contest. The vampire was a sure winner. They liked the way he looked, even if he couldn't sing very well. Too bad he wasn't going to be there to collect.

Then Elvis had a thought. He opened the CD compartment on the Bose and looked at the selections on the disc.

"Hold on a minute," he called to the announcer. "I think I'd like to give it a try."

"All right," the announcer said. "Let's give this man a hand." Elvis walked to the stage. "And what's your name, sir?"

Elvis hesitated, but not for long. "King," he said. "Aaron King. That's Aaron with two A's."

The announcer laughed. "Let's hear it then, for the King, for Aaron with two A's!"

There was almost no applause at all, but Elvis didn't care. He turned on the Bose and began belting out "One Night," not the sanitized version that he'd released on RCA but the real one, the one he'd learned from the old Smiley Lewis 78, all about the one night of sin he was now payin' for.

It was as if the years dropped away as soon as the first note of music came out of the machine, as if he'd never stopped performing. He'd never sung better. His hips had never moved more smoothly. He'd never meant anything more than he meant the words to the song.

The applause started before he even finished. There were women bouncing in their chairs and screaming so loud that their dates and husbands looked disgusted, but even they were clapping.

He could hear one woman yelling to her companion, "He don't look a *thing* like Elvis, but lordy he can *sing!*"

It's just as good as it ever was, Elvis thought. "They sustain me." Wasn't that what the vampire had said? Elvis looked around at the small but madly clapping crowd. Suddenly he knew exactly how he would be spending the rest of his life, and he grinned. He was going to be pretty damn good at impersonating himself.

"Thank yew," he drawled, bowing to the crowd. "Thank yew ver' much. Thank yew."

He had his two hundred and fifty dollars in his billfold and he was standing in the parking lot where the vampire had been.

There was nothing left there now except maybe a little of the dirt that had come from the medallion, but the breeze was strong from the south and most of the dirt and dust had blown away. Even the jumpsuit was gone, and Elvis wondered if someone had picked it up for a souvenir. Probably had. He wasn't interested in it himself. He was going to be the Young Elvis.

He tossed the Bose into the back seat of the Caddy and drove out of the parking lot. He'd heard there was a contest scheduled in L.A. in a couple of weeks. Might as well head that way right now.

When he was gliding along the interstate, he looked to his left and saw the hotel outlined against the night sky. "Ladies and gentlemen," he said, flooring the accelerator and looking back through the windshield toward the west, toward California, "Elvis has left the building."

This story was nominated for an Anthony Award for "best short story." Naturally, I'm very fond of it, and I especially like the title.

How I Found a Cat, Lost True Love, and Broke the Bank at Monte Carlo

1

Actually, the cat found me.

I was in the market section of Monaco, between the hills that support the royal palace on the one hand and the casino section of Monte Carlo on the other. It was a lovely day in early fall, the kind you read about in tourist manuals. The sun was bright, and the sky was a hard, brilliant blue.

The market was so crowded that I could hardly move. Flower vendors offered red and yellow and white blossoms that overflowed their paper cones, while food vendors hawked fish and vegetables, fruit and pastries. Shoppers swirled around me, and the street was packed with cars and vans.

The smells of roses and freshly-caught seafood mingled with the odor of coffee from the sidewalk cafes, and I was thinking about having a cup of mocha when the cat ran up my leg, digging its claws into my jeans and hoisting itself right up to my waist.

For some reason I've never understood, cats find me attractive.

I settled my glasses on my nose, gently pried the cat loose

and held her in my arms. She was mostly black, with a white streak on her nose, a white badge on her chest, and white socks on her legs. Her eyes were emerald green, and her heart was pounding as if she were frightened, but in that mob it was hard to tell what might be scaring her.

"What's the matter, cat?" I asked. Maybe that's why cats like me. I treat them as if their brains were larger than walnuts, though they aren't.

The cat of course didn't answer, but she did seem to relax a bit. Then a dog barked somewhere nearby and the cat tensed up, sliding her claws out and through my shirt, into the skin of my chest.

"It's all right," I said, squirming a little. "I won't let the dog get you."

The cat looked wide-eyed out over the heads of the crowd for the source of the barking. There was no dog in evidence, and though the cat didn't appear entirely convinced of my ability to protect her, she withdrew her claws from my shirt.

I hadn't come to Monaco to adopt a cat, as attractive as that idea might seem, so I looked around for someone to take her off my hands.

That's when I saw the woman.

She wasn't just any woman. She was *the* woman. Even in that crowd of the rich and beautiful she stood out. She was tall and lithe. Her hair was midnight black under a pink sun hat, and her eyes were as deeply green as those of the cat I held in my arms. And she was walking straight toward me.

I was in love.

I opened my mouth, but nothing came out. Truly beautiful women affect my nervous system. They might not often be attracted to me, but I was certainly attracted to them.

"Hello," she said in English. She had that unidentifiable continental accent that I'd heard a lot in the last few days, but somehow it seemed much more charming from her than it had from anyone else. "Are you American?"

I managed to get my mouth to work. "How did you know?"

She laughed, though it was more like music to me than laughter. "You Americans are all alike. There is such an innocence about you."

She reached for the cat and rubbed a white hand along its dark coat. The cat began purring.

"That is why animals trust you," she said. "They can sense the innocence."

"I wondered about that," I told her.

"I'm sure that you did. True innocence never knows itself."

She took the cat from me. It went quite willingly and settled into her arms as if it belonged there.

"I thank you very much for rescuing Michelle. My uncle and I came to the market for fish, and she escaped my car when I opened the door to leave. There was a dog nearby, and I suspect that his barking may have frightened her."

"We heard him," I said.

She started to turn away, which is usually the case with women I meet. But then something unusual happened. She turned back.

"Would you like a cup of coffee, perhaps? Michelle would like to repay you for the rescue."

"What about your uncle?" I asked. Somehow I managed it without stuttering. "Won't he be worried about the cat?"

"He won't mind. He'll find us, I'm sure."

"I'd love some coffee," I said.

It was just as noisy at the small table where we sat under a striped umbrella as it had been in the market, but somehow we seemed isolated in an island of quiet where the only sounds were our two voices, along with the occasional mew from Michelle, who sat on a chair beside her owner, whose name was Antoinette Sagan. Tony, to her friends, of which I was now officially one.

I had already told her to call me Mike.

"And what are you doing here in Monaco?" Tony asked me as she sipped her coffee.

"I came to break the bank at the casino," I said, pushing up my glasses.

Tony set her cup down and laughed. "As so many have. And how do you plan to do so?"

"Roulette," I said. "I have a system."

Tony winked at the cat. "Do you hear that, Michelle? The American has a system."

Michelle wasn't interested. She was watching some kind of bug that was crawling along the walk just beneath her chair.

Tony looked back at me and smiled. The green of her eyes was amazing. I think my heart fibrillated.

"Everyone has a system," she said. "For cards, for dice, for roulette. They come to Monaco daily. But no one has ever broken the bank."

"You'd never know if someone did," I said. "They'd never tell, and the banks here know how to keep a secret. Anyway, I don't have to break the bank, not really. I'd settle for a few million dollars."

Michelle had lost interest in the bug. She stepped up on the table and walked across it to me. She climbed into my lap, turned in a circle and lay down, purring loudly.

"I believe you've made a conquest," Tony said. "And what is your system, if I may ask? Or is it a secret?"

I told her it wasn't a secret. I took one of my pens out of my pocket protector and pulled a napkin across the table.

"Do you know the game?" I asked.

Tony shrugged. The white shirt moved in interesting places, but I tried to ignore that.

"Of course," she said.

"Then you know the odds favoring the house." I jotted them on the napkin. "In American roulette, the house edge is 5.26%; in the European version it's 2.70% because there's no double zero on the wheel."

"So of course you'll be playing the European version."

"Of course. Now. Have you ever heard of the Martingale system?"

Tony made a comic frown. "Who has not? Many millions of francs have been lost with it. You make your bet. If you win, you take your winnings and begin again. If you lose, you double the bet. Lose again, double again." She took the pen from my hand and began scribbling on the napkin. "Say that your bet is 100 francs on red. Seven times in a row the wheel comes up black. That means that your next bet will be 12,800 francs, but you will have already lost 12,700 francs. Should you win, you win 100 francs, should you lose. . . ." She shrugged again. "The *croupier* will be overjoyed to have you at his table."

Her figures were correct, and of course the house odds defeat everyone in the long run. I was going to beat the odds.

I told Tony that I was a math teacher at a community college in the States. That I'd always been fascinated with odds and statistics. And that I'd recently won fifty thousand dollars in the state lottery.

"Winning such a large amount was very lucky," she said. "And you have come to Monaco to lose it all at the roulette table? That does not seem practical."

"I'm not practical, and I don't think I'm going to lose."

I tried to elaborate on my system, which I explained was an elegant variation on the Martingale, involving shifting the bet to different locations, avoiding the low payoffs like red or black while never trying for the larger payoffs like the single number bet, and even dropping out of the betting occasionally.

"And if all else fails," I said, "maybe I'll get lucky."

"It has happened," she said.

"Right. About eighty years ago, black came up seventeen times in a row on one table. Anyone starting out with a dollar and leaving it on black would have won over, let's see. . . ." I worked it out on the napkin. "One hundred thirty-one thousand, seventy-two dollars. It could happen to me."

She looked at the cat, which was still lying comfortably in my lap. "You seem like a nice man, Mike. I hope it does happen to you, and that you pick up your money before the eighteenth spin of the wheel."

Her smile made my knees weak.

"I could share it with you if it happens that way," I said, hardly caring that her answer could pose a real problem for me if it was the one I wanted to hear.

She opened her mouth to say something, but I never found out what it was. She saw someone behind me, and her eyes darkened. She closed her mouth.

I looked around. A very large man stood there. He wore a white shirt and dark slacks, and he had a dark face that was pitted like volcanic rock. I suppose you could call him ruggedly handsome if you liked the type.

Tony said, "Hello, Andre. This is Mike. He has found Michelle."

I picked up the cat in my left arm and began to turn. Michelle growled low in her throat, and the hair ridged along her back.

"Stupid cat," Andre said. His voice was like Michelle's growl.

"Andre is my uncle," Tony explained. "He and Michelle are not mutual admirers."

I could see that much. I could also see that Andre was not at all interested in meeting me, much less in shaking hands. I dropped the hand that I had been about to extend.

Tony came around the table and took Michelle, who had stopped growling, though she didn't look very happy.

"Thank you so much, Mike," Tony said. "Andre and I are both grateful."

Sure they were. Andre had already turned his back and was walking away. He was wide as a billboard.

"I hope you win at the casino," Tony said over her shoulder as she turned to follow Andre.

I watched them move through the crowd. Andre didn't look like anyone's uncle to me, and I wondered if Tony had lied. I suppose that it didn't make any difference.

Besides, if she had lied, we were even. After all, I hadn't won the lottery. I wasn't even a math teacher.

2

Cammie was waiting for me in a little cafe not far from the market. She was drinking black coffee and smoking a Players. She knew I didn't like cigarettes, but she didn't bother to snuff it out when I sat down. No one else minded. It wasn't like an American cafe. There were lots of smokers.

It was a little after noon, and I ordered a sandwich. Cammie didn't want one. She was too wired to eat.

"You look really dorky in those glasses," she said. Her voice was low and slightly husky, a quality I attributed to the cigarettes. "And where on earth did you get the pocket pro-tector? 'Elmer's Plumbing'? Give me a break."

"I thought it was a nice touch," I told her.

She took a deep swallow of coffee. "You probably think that stupid part in your hair's a nice touch, too, but it isn't."

"It should fool the *croupier*," I said. "He won't know he's seen me before."

"I guess. If you want to risk it."

"I'm willing. What did you find out?"

She blew a spiral of smoke and looked around. No one appeared interested in us.

"I think you were right," she said, grinning.

She looked good with a grin. Short blonde hair, blue eyes, a small mouth and nose. Sort of the gaming look. Not that she looked as good as Tony, but she looked pretty good.

And like me, she could look quite different when the occasion called for it, as it had lately. Yesterday she'd looked like a fashion model on vacation, and the day before that she'd looked like a harassed mother who'd misplaced her three kids.

We'd been watching the wheels in Monte Carlo's famous casino for four days, and we'd settled on the one at table four a couple of days earlier. My theory was that a system wasn't good enough. It would help if you could find a wheel that was just slightly out of balance.

It didn't need to be out of balance much. Hardly any, in fact, and the odds against finding one were quite high in themselves. Casinos generally go to a lot of trouble to make sure that everything is perfect, but now and then someone slips up. It doesn't happen often. Hardly ever, in fact. But it does happen.

We'd been looking for weeks. Monte Carlo wasn't our first stop, and it wouldn't have been our last had we not found the right wheel. It looked like we had.

All we needed was a wheel that turned up one number more often than any other. To be sure that we'd found one, we had to watch it for at least twenty-four hours. We'd been watching for forty-eight, spread out over three days, in our various disguises. Cammie had just come off the final shift.

"So it's the red five?" I said.

She crushed out the cigarette. "It's the red five all right. Table four."

The odds of any single number coming up are one in thirty-seven. The red five was coming up more often than that, more like one time in thirty. That was more than often enough to offset the house odds on a single zero wheel.

"So if they don't adjust the wheel before tonight, we use the system on the red five," she said. "At table four. And you're the player."

"That's me. Joe Nerd."

"You're not going to wear that get-up. Not really."

I told her that I wasn't going to change much, and that I had a good reason. When I told her why, she wasn't happy with me.

"You idiot! You actually *told* someone we had a system?"

"Not *we*. I told her that *I* had a system. She doesn't know about you. And I didn't tell her anything at all about the wheel. So don't worry."

Cammie showed instant suspicion, one of her less attractive qualities. "I should have known it was a woman. You always talk too much to women. What does she look like?"

The waiter brought my sandwich, and I took a bite to avoid answering. After I'd finished chewing, I said, "She looks good. But not great."

Cammie narrowed her eyes. I could tell she didn't trust me, not that I blamed her.

Cammie and I had met two years earlier in Las Vegas,

where she'd been dealing blackjack. I'd made a bundle at her table, and we'd gotten out of town just before anyone figured out how I was doing it, a little matter of a trick that involved her help and that was in violation of every casino rule in the book. We'd made a little money since, here and there, enough so that I had a pretty good stake, and then I'd come up with the idea of finding a roulette wheel that was just slightly out of whack. I'd never expected to find it in Monte Carlo, really, but I was just as happy that we had.

"So why did you tell her?" Cammie asked. "I thought you were nervous around women."

She knew me pretty well. I'd been nervous around her, too, at first, and talked too much, though if I hadn't had a drink or three too many, I'd never have tried to con her into helping me with the blackjack scam. As it turned out, she didn't need conning. She was eager to help.

"I found her cat," I said. I told her all about Tony, the cat, and Uncle Andre.

"Uncle, my aunt fanny," she said. She got out a Players and lit it with a disposable lighter from her purse. "You should've kept your mouth shut."

"Not really," I rationalized. "That's the beauty of it. She seems to know her way around here, and when word gets out that some geek broke the bank, she'll remember me and tell people about my supposed 'system.' People will think I got lucky. No one will ever know we had a fixed wheel."

"It isn't fixed. It's just a little out of balance."

"You're absolutely right. And they certainly can't blame us for that."

She blew a smoke ring and stuck her finger through it. "Describe this Andre for me again."

I did.

"Dark hair?"

For some reason, I don't usually notice men's hair, but now that she mentioned it, I remembered.

"Yes," I said. "And a little curly."

"I think I've seen him around the casino. Do you think he could be security?"

He was certainly big enough, but I didn't think they'd use anyone that obvious.

"Probably just another gambler," I said. "And remember what we just discussed. It's not our fault if the wheel's out of balance."

She took a deep drag from the cigarette and turned to blow the smoke away from me. Or maybe she just didn't want me to see her face.

"I'll remember," she said.

3

I went to the casino just as night was falling. I had to walk, because parking in the crush of automobiles there is almost impossible, but I didn't mind. The casino is an impressive sight, worth looking at as you approach it from nearly any angle, especially at night when the floodlights are on.

The floodlights brighten the ornate casino facade and throw into obscurity the high-rises that suffocate the area around it. Once, Monte Carlo must have been a beautiful place, but now it looks a lot like any city anywhere.

Across from the casino, boats lined the harbor, and there was just the faintest tinge of azure still in the sky where it met the dark sea.

I had on my thick-rimmed glasses, and I was wearing a dark three-piece suit that was about four years out of style, loafers with tassels, and a paisley tie. I was worth a second glance from the man who checked my passport, but no more than that. He didn't care how I dressed as long as I had on a tie.

He returned my passport, and I walked into the American Room, which is filled with tourists who seem to want to lose their money fast. The smoky air was noisy with the sound of the one hundred and twenty slot machines and the balls clacking around the American-style roulette wheels.

I walked right on through, with only a glance into the Pink Salon, the bar where Cammie would be waiting for me. The ceiling was painted with floating women, most of whom were nude and most of whom were smoking. I didn't see Cammie.

As I paid my fee to enter the European Gaming Room, I had a qualm or two about the tie and about the tassels on the loafers; the standards here were somewhat higher than for the first room in the casino. But apparently I passed muster. I was allowed to enter.

Besides being classier, the European Room was much quieter than the American Room. Nearly everyone was better dressed than I was, and everyone looked quite serious about the business at hand, which was gambling. The *chefs* watched the tables from tall wooden chairs, their eyes bright and alert for any sign of trouble.

I wasn't going to be any trouble. I was just there to win a large sum of money. I exchanged a huge wad of francs for chips and walked up to the table, which was set up a bit differently from an American table. There are layouts for betting on both sides of the table, and in this room there were padded rails not far away so that onlookers could lean at their ease and get a few vicarious thrills by watching the real gamblers.

I approached the table and put five hundred francs down on the black ten. I thought I might as well lose a little to begin with.

Almost as soon as the money was down, one of the *croupiers* said, *"Rien ne va plus."* The *tourneur* spun the wheel and dropped the silver ball, which whirred and bounced and clicked. I took a deep breath and waited for it to drop.

I don't know when Tony arrived. I noticed her about two hours into the game, standing at the rail directly across the table from me. She smiled when I looked up, and my concentration broke for a moment.

That was all right. I needed a little break. I was almost 50,000 francs in the hole. It wasn't as bad as it sounds at first, since a dollar is worth five francs, but 10,000 dollars is still a lot of money. In fact it was about a third of my stake. Things weren't working out exactly as I'd planned.

The red five hadn't been coming up, not often enough and certainly not when I had money on it. My real plan—as opposed to the one I'd told Tony about—had been to move the money around at first, putting a little on the red five now and then so that no one would be suspicious when I started playing the five exclusively. I'd win a little, lose a little, then get hot and break the bank.

It had seemed like a good plan when I thought of it, but obviously it wasn't working out. I was losing more than I was winning. Maybe the wheel wasn't out of balance after all. Or maybe I was just unlucky.

There was a TV commercial in the states when I left, something about never letting them see you sweat. Well, I was sweating, and if something good didn't happen soon, they were going to see me doing it.

The break was over. I wondered if Tony's appearance at the rail might not be an omen. What the hell, I thought. I shoved all the rest of my chips out on the table, onto the red five.

The *tourneur* gave the wheel a practiced spin and flipped the ball in the opposite direction. Time suddenly slowed down. The ball glided like mercury on tile, and then it began bouncing. Every time that it bounced, it seemed to hang in the air for several seconds before striking the wheel again.

I looked at Tony. She was still smiling; it was as if she hadn't moved at all.

I glanced back at the wheel, and things suddenly snapped back to normal. The ball bounced once, twice, three times, and landed in the red five.

As the *croupier* called out the number, I let out a breath that I hadn't even known I was holding. I'd put nearly 25,000 francs on the number, at odds of thirty-five to one. That meant I'd won almost 175,000 dollars in one spin of the wheel.

I straightened my glasses. "Let it ride," I said. It was time to go with the flow.

The *croupier* called to someone, and a man dressed better than most of the gamblers came over to the table. There was a whispered conversation.

I thought about the time all those years ago when the ball had landed in the black seventeen times in a row. I didn't need seventeen times in a row. I just needed to hit one more time. The odds against it happening were huge, but not as bad as you might think. The wheel didn't know that the red five had just come up. I had the same chance of hitting it again that I'd had the first time. And if the wheel really was out of balance, maybe the chance was better than it should be.

The *croupier* was looking at me as the well-dressed man whispered to him. I tried to keep my voice level and repeated, "Let it ride."

The man was finished with the *croupier*. Now he wanted to

talk to me. I didn't blame him. If I hit, I was going to win something like six and a quarter million dollars. I was sweating a lot more now than I'd been when I was losing.

The man was very polite, and he didn't appear to be as nervous as I was. Probably he dealt with large sums of money more often than I did.

"Are you enjoying yourself, *monsieur?*" he asked.

"Very much," I said, taking off my glasses and cleaning them with a tissue from my suit pocket. My heart was about to jump out of my chest, but my hands didn't tremble. Much.

"Do you realize the value of your bet?" His voice was as calm as if he were discussing the beautiful autumn weather we were having.

"I believe I do," I said, settling the glasses on my nose and returning the tissue to my pocket. I patted my hair just to the right of the part and smiled at him.

"You have won quite a sum of money already. Are you sure that you want to risk it all on one spin of the wheel?"

I shrugged. Casual Joe Nerd. "Easy come, easy go."

He mumbled something then that might have been a reference to "stupid Americans," but I didn't quite catch it. I wasn't meant to.

I looked around at the crowd. There were a lot more people watching now than there had been only moments before. All of them were observing us expectantly, Tony among them. She licked her lips in anticipation, and my heart beat even faster.

"Everyone's waiting," I said. "I hope the casino won't let them down."

The man didn't bother to look at the crowd. For that matter, he didn't bother to look at me. Six million dollars wasn't really that much money, not to him and the house. It wouldn't break the bank, though it would come close enough to satisfy me.

The man nodded to the *croupier*, who said, *"Rien ne va plus."* The room became as silent as an empty cathedral.

When the *tourneur* spun the wheel, it seemed to roar like a jet plane on take-off. The ball zipped around like an Indy racer, and when it bounced it sounded like a skull ricocheting inside a marble cavern.

I couldn't watch. I closed my eyes. I may even have crossed my fingers.

About ten years later, I heard the *croupier*.

"Cinc." There was a pause of nearly a century, and I could hear the blood pounding in my head. Then he said, quite calmly, *"Rouge."*

I opened my eyes. There was a clamoring and shouting like you might hear when an underdog wins the Super Bowl. Men were pounding me on the back and women were trying to kiss me. My knees were weak, but I was rapidly gaining strength.

I craned my neck above the sea of heads, trying to find Tony, but she was gone. I didn't wonder about her for long. Instead I looked back at the wheel and the silvery ball nestling in the red five.

I'll admit it. There was an instant when I actually thought about saying, "Let it ride." If I hit again, I'd win over 214 million dollars. I really would break the bank at Monte Carlo, or come very close.

Would the well-dressed man have let me take the chance? Probably, in the hope that I'd lose; the odds were certainly against me, unbalanced wheel or not. Or maybe he'd hustle me outside, unwilling to allow me the opportunity to win.

It didn't matter. I told them to cash me in.

"Follow me, *monsieur*," the well-dressed man said. I did,

after making sure that the *croupiers* and the *tourneur* had nice tips. I could afford to be generous.

I couldn't resist looking back, though, to see where the ball landed on the next spin.

In the black, thirty-two.

It was just as well I'd stopped.

4

Cammie was in the bar when I arrived carrying a black leather case.

"My God," she said. "You won."

I nodded.

She crushed out the cigarette she had been smoking, a sure sign that she was excited. "How much?" She didn't wait for an answer. "Was that cheering I heard in there for you? I thought it might be, but I couldn't bear to go in and find out."

I said that the cheering was for me.

"Oh my God! I can't believe it! How much?"

I told her.

She stared at the leather bag. "And it's all in there?"

"Not all of it. They don't keep that much on hand, or if they do, they don't give it out to guys like me. But there's a lot. I told them I'd take a check for the rest."

"My God." She fumbled in her purse for her cigarettes, then gave it up. She looked back at the bag. "Everyone in that room knows you won. How are we going to get it to the hotel without being robbed?"

I turned and gestured toward the doorway. There were two large men in tight suits standing there.

"The casino was kind enough to provide an escort. No one

wants to see a lucky gambler lose his winnings to a footpad."

"A footpad?"

"Cutpurse, mugger, what-have-you."

"You talk funny when you're excited."

"If you think I'm excited now, wait until we get to the hotel. I've always wanted to play Scrooge McDuck. You know. Throw it up and let it hit me on the head. Burrow through it like a gopher."

"Now's your chance," she said. She hooked an arm through mine. "Let's go."

We arrived at the hotel without incident, and the bodyguards left us without a word, except to thank me for the tip. I was about to have the bag put in the hotel vault when Cammie stopped me.

"Scrooge McDuck," she said. "Remember?"

I didn't suppose it would hurt anything. She deserved to see the money. And the check. We went up to the room.

When we opened the door, we got quite a surprise.

Tony was sitting in an armchair, waiting for us. So was Michelle, who was curled in Tony's lap, asleep.

And so, unfortunately, was Uncle Andre, who was holding a very ugly pistol in his right hand. A Glock 17, ugly but very accurate, or so I've heard.

"Shit," Cammie said, glaring at me. I didn't blame her.

"Close the door," Andre said, moving the pistol barrel just slightly.

I did what he said.

"Who's your friend, Mike?" Tony asked.

"Inspector Lestrade, Scotland Yard," I said, but no one laughed.

"You're a very lucky man, Mike," Tony said, stroking Michelle's back. The cat began to purr so loudly that I could hear her across the room. "Didn't I tell you he seemed lucky, Andre?"

"If I were lucky, you wouldn't be here," I said, thinking that it was really too bad. She was such a beautiful woman, and I'd been halfway in love with her. If she'd asked me nicely, I might have given her the money; after all, in a way, she'd helped me win it. Then again, maybe I wouldn't have.

Andre didn't seem to care one way or the other. "Give me the bag," he said.

"It won't do you any good," Cammie said. "There's no money. It's a check."

"I'm afraid we don't believe that," Tony said. "You see, we've been waiting around for days for someone like you, Mike. Andre is a terrible gambler, and I am not much better, but I could tell this morning that you were different. Did I not say so, Andre?"

Andre said nothing. He just stared at me with eyes like black glass.

"I had to ask Andre to wait. He wanted to take you for a little ride this morning and relieve you of your stake, but I told him to wait. I told him I had faith in you. Is that not true, Andre?"

Andre didn't answer the question. "Give me the bag," he told me, "or I will shoot your woman."

Cammie was furious. With me, for having told Tony I had a system, and with Andre for calling her my woman.

"He won't shoot," she said. "If he does, half the hotel will come running to this room."

"That is true," Tony said.

She got up, carrying the cat along with her, and walked to the bed. She picked up one of the pillows and took it to Andre.

"Use this," she said.

Andre muffled the pistol with the pillow. "Give me the bag."

I tensed just a little.

"And don't throw it," Andre said. "I'll shoot your woman."

"Shoot me then, you son of a bitch," Cammie said, throwing her purse at him.

When she did, I swung the bag as hard as I could at Tony. I hated to mess up her beautiful face, but I didn't hate it as much as I hated the thought of giving them any of my money.

The bag hit Tony at just about the same time the pistol went off, and made just about as much noise.

Even noisier than the pistol was the cat, which had jumped from Tony's arms and was yowling in the middle of the floor, its back arched, its tail puffed to three times its normal size. The air was filled with feathers from the pillow. I couldn't see Cammie. Maybe she had taken cover in the bathroom.

Tony had fallen back across the bed. Her nose was bleeding, but I wasn't worried about her. I was worried about Andre, who had started toward me. He wouldn't need the pistol. He could break me in half with his bare hands if he wanted to.

He might have done it, but he made one mistake. He didn't watch out for the cat. Maybe he didn't see her because of the feathers.

Michelle didn't like him anyway, and when he ran into her, she fastened herself to his right leg, sinking her claws into his calf and trying to bite through his pants.

He was hopping on his left leg and pointing the pistol at her when I let him have it with the bag. His face was one I didn't mind messing up.

I connected solidly, and Andre staggered backward. Michelle released him and ran under the bed, which was just as well. When I hit Andre again, he wobbled against the French doors that led to a tiny balcony.

The doors weren't locked, and they hardly slowed him down. Neither did the low railing outside. I have to give him credit. He didn't yell as he went over, or even on the way down. I heard him crash into some patio furniture.

I went outside and looked down. Andre was sprawled atop the remains of a metal table. Our room was on the third floor, not so great a distance from the ground. Maybe he'd even survive.

I heard a noise and turned back to the room. Tony was still on the bed, but now Cammie was sitting on top of her, straddling her waist. Tony was struggling to get up, but Cammie had pinned her arms and all she could do was thrash around.

"Let her go," I said. "She won't bother us without Andre around."

Cammie got off Tony, though I could tell she wanted to do a little more damage first. She stood beside the bed, disheveled and glowering. Her nose was no longer bleeding, however.

"Are you all right?" I asked Tony.

"You brogue my dose, you sud of a bitch."

Cammie, either because she felt sorry for Tony or because she didn't like the sight of blood, got her purse from the floor and dug around until she found a couple of tissues. She handed them to Tony.

"Sorry about your nose," I said. "You were trying to rob me, after all. Is that what you and Andre do for a living? Rob innocent tourists?"

She crumpled the tissues. "Iddocedt? Whod's iddocedt, you sud of a—"

"Never mind," I said. "And you don't have to call us names. We're not going to turn you in."

"We're not?" Cammie said.

"We don't want to cause any trouble. We just want to go on our way and enjoy our money. And we have lots to enjoy."

Tony sat up. She was wearing a white blouse, and there was a lot of blood on it. I wondered what the hotel staff would make of that, but I decided I didn't care.

"I cad go?" she said.

"Sure. Don't let us keep you. And you might want to check on your friend. I'm not sure, but I thought I saw him moving."

She stalked across the room. When her hand touched the doorknob, Cammie said, "Don't forget your cat."

"Andre has never liked Michelle," Tony said. "I do not think he will want to see her again."

And then she was out the door and gone.

Cammie took a deep breath. "You always talk too much to women," she said.

"And you smoke too much. I'll try to quit talking too much to women if you'll try to stop smoking."

I still had the bag in my hand. I walked over and put it on the chair. I thought it would be a good idea to put the money in the hotel safe now. I was no longer in the mood to play Scrooge McDuck.

"Why all the sudden concern about my smoking?" Cammie asked.

Michelle came halfway out from under the bed and stared at us. After a second or two she walked over and started rubbing against my leg and purring.

"Second-hand smoke," I said, reaching down to stroke Michelle's head. She began to purr even louder. Cats liked me, all right. "It's bad for the cat."